The Gentleman on Pennyfield Street

The Gentleman on Pennyfield Street

Dory Sparks Series Book Three
By C.G. Oster

The Gentleman on Pennyfield Street

Chapter 1

September 1940

IN HER LIGHT GREEN uniform, Dory Sparks walked out of the small brick house she shared with a few of the other girls working at the Chiswell munitions factory. Lorries trundled along the street to the factory located at the edge of town. It was a sprawling complex with two tall chimneys belching black smoke.

The dust and dirt got into everything and she didn't have any nails left for the sticky TNT to hide under. The smell of it made her wash her hair every day and she was getting used to sleeping with perpetually wet hair when she came home late in the evenings. Either that or wash black dirt off her sheets every other day.

It was hard work. They worked every day of the week and got only two days off per month, but it was necessary work—if monotonously boring. It paid well, particularly in her group. She was group eight, tasked with handling the amatol which turned the mortars from innocent steel tubes into proper explosives.

Filing in through the gates with the crowd of other girls, Dory found her timesheet and shoved it into the punch. As she walked, people melted away to their workstations, she toward the far end where the filling operations were, separated by a thick concrete wall from the storage area, where workers were classified at the most dangerous level.

It was strongly encouraged that you were unmarried to work in the higher levels, in case things went wrong—and when things went wrong, they went spectacularly wrong. One munition going off was bad enough, but one exploding set off all the other ones around it and then the building was more or less pulverized. So it wasn't a place to be careless.

Reaching the filling part of the factory, Dory moved to her workspace, where ordinates were already lined up, ready to be filled. Her job was to go to the smelter, where the amatol was heated and to carry it over to the ordinates, fill and attach the detonators. Others then transferred the ordinates to the storage area, where they never waited around too long.

The factory worked at full capacity. The need for ordinates meant that no slack in production was allowed.

Through the grubby glass window, Dory saw what looked like a lovely autumn day pass by. Her hands were red and uncomfortable inside the leather gloves she wore and sweat ran down her back from the constant lifting and heaving.

Placing her bucket down, she grabbed the wooden stick and went from one mortar to the next, gently stirring the amatol inside the drilled barrel. Any air pockets made the mortar explode in the tube, probably killing some young lad in the process.

It was hard to think about what all these mortars would be used for. War was triage. It was better them than us, and at times Dory wondered how in the world they had got themselves into this situation. The world was unrecognizable, but she worked as hard as she could to produce the ordinates that would kill the enemy.

At times, she thought back longingly on the still and peaceful days in St. Tropez. They seemed a lifetime away, even if it had actually been less than a year. Here, one day was much like another. Rise at dawn, work until well into the evening and try to sleep in between—with wet hair.

On her days off, she went to the pictures. A moment of escape, but first she had to sit through the Pathé pictures which showed overly enthusiastic depictions of the national pride. Sometimes Dory wondered if there were some who were excited about the unfolding developments of this war. It sounded that way, according to how upbeat the news presenters were.

Hollywood always came through with an escape, with glamorous dresses and handsome men in some comedy of errors. A place far away where there was no war.

There were war movies as well, but Dory didn't go to those. There was enough bravery in the girls around her. She didn't need to know how brave their men were. It was too frightening.

Recently, she had written to DI Ridley, wishing him the best of luck for all the endeavors he faced, knowing he could tell her very little of what he did with Military Intelligence. It could be that he didn't even receive her letter.

More regularly, she wrote to Lady Pettifer, who was back at Wallisford Hall with her brother. Part of the estate had been given over to the Ministry of Food to raise chickens. Dory couldn't imagine the grand estate with countless chicken coops. Livinia, Lady Pettifer's niece, was apparently working as a secretary at the Ministry of War. It seemed everyone had to do their effort for the war.

"Miss Sparks," a voice said, breaking into Dory's thoughts. "Please come to the office immediately."

The woman in a tight pencil skirt and heels walked away. Judging by her dress, not one of the factory workers—instead from the administration office.

Dory had no idea what this could be about, but she finished screwing on the last of the caps and indicated to the man from storage that he could move the lot in front of her.

At the sink, she washed her hands with the large, gritty bar of soap, trying to get as much of the dirt off. Even with gloves, it got all over her hands. With a sigh, she looked at her hands and gave up.

It was a long walk back to the office, past large machining equipment. The woman hadn't even said her name and Dory wasn't sure she would recognize her face.

The office was crowded with small desks, the cackle from the typewriters filling her ears. Dory walked toward a desk where she thought she recognized a girl. "I'm Dory Sparks. Someone wished to see me."

The girl looked up and adjusted her glasses, staring incomprehensively. Wonderful, Dory thought. She had no idea where to go.

"This way, Miss Sparks," someone called and Dory turned to see the tight pencil skirt again. It was a lovely skirt. Dory wished she had one. The woman walked down a corridor and Dory followed. "In here."

"Right," Dory said and took off the handkerchief that held back her hair. The room was small with a table in the middle, two women in dark green uniforms sitting by the table, their heads down in a file. "Miss Sparks?" the older woman said as she looked up.

"Yes."

"Please sit," she said, indicating to the chair on the other side of the table. "Now, you're a group eight I understand."

"Yes."

"I am Marjorie Dam from the ATS," she said with a smile. The ATS was the Auxiliary Territorial Services. Their posters were intermittently plastered up around town, along with the WRENs and the WAAF. "We are looking for girls with strong nerves and you obviously have to have doing the job you do." The woman twisted her head to the side as she considered Dory. The other woman was watching her intently too. "I think you might be exactly what we are looking for."

"Oh, yes?" Dory said, not having enough information to really understand what these people wanted. In truth, she had little understanding of what the ATS did, or the others.

"Are you interested in performing a more active role in the war?"

Dory wasn't sure if she could give any more than she already was, working every hour of the day as she was. "You mean go to France?"

"No, nothing like that."

"We're looking for women to help with our home defenses."

The other woman started speaking. "As you know, the Germans have their bombing raids across the southern parts, particularly London. We need to bolster our defenses."

"We need someone with a bit of nerve."

Which meant there was some risk involved. "I'm listening."

"Excellent. We are specifically talking about anti-aircraft defenses."

"The guns that fire at the enemy planes," Dory said.

"Not the guns exactly. We represent more the detection."

"Specifically in London," the other woman filled in.

Dory blinked. London was where the raids were, so it made sense that was where the detection was. But they had also come all the way up here to search for people as opposed to selecting from the numerous women in London.

"You are unmarried," one of the women said, consulting the file, which meant there was definitely risk involved.

"Yes."

"Training is provided. You will perform a very vital function for your country and would do your bit to stop the bombings that are devastating London."

Obviously, she could say no, but could she live with herself? If not the guns, then Dory guessed they were looking for women to man the searchlights, which meant being active and vulnerable when the enemy aircrafts were over London—when the bombs were dropping.

Perhaps it as understandable that they recruited from factories where women were already performing dangerous roles.

"The hours are unsociable," the woman continued. "The Germans have changed their tactics and come more at night now than they did before."

"I see," Dory said.

"It would be awfully good if you could join us, Miss Sparks. Our boys could use all the support they can get, but our populace need defending too. You can play a real and vital role in that."

With a sigh, Dory stroked her hands down her cheeks toward her mouth. "Of course," she said.

"Excellent. Now you need to travel to Preston in Lancashire, where you can enlist and receive the King's shilling."

The notion sounded outlandish—positively medieval—but she was being pressed into service.

"Obviously, there will be a physical exam, but I don't expect you will have any problems. Here is a voucher for travel. Simply present it to the stationmaster and he should put you on the next train heading in the right direction. So pleased you are considering joining us. With women like yourself, this war can be won." She tore a yellow piece of paper from a booklet and handed it over to Dory.

Dory looked down on it, where in black print it said the holder could travel to Preston, Lancashire from anywhere in the country. "Thank you," she said, not feeling the certainty that these two women projected.

Already, though, Dory knew she couldn't say no. The army had come all the way up here to ask her to join. It would prey on her until the end of her days if she declined. So, no more working in the factory.

Instead, she would have to face the bombs dropping on London.

Chapter 2

"TRY TEN DEGREES EAST," Vera called, training her binoculars eastwards. The drone of coming aircrafts was unmistakable.

Tight dread gripped Dory's heart as she quickly turned the wheel that shifted the massive arc light. Heat steamed off the light and burned into one side of her body as she turned the heavy wheel. One wheel made it go up and down and another side to side.

The aircrafts were coming closer and Dory moved the wheels to find one. They were difficult to find, but when she did, they lit up like silver coins in the dark sky. Catching something, she had to go back and the bofor gun across the river started firing, then another, the steady percussions of the high caliber bullets echoing toward them. The hot bullets flew up in the sky, by illusions sometimes looking like swooping starlings.

From the sounds of the droning engines, a whole squadron of German—Heinkels if she were to guess. Closer and closer they came, then the sickening whistle of the bombs. Constantly they were listening for the ones that seemed to grow endlessly louder. The explosions started, lighting the sky like fireworks. They always fell in twos, mere seconds apart. It was a terrible beauty these nights.

Dory swung the heavy arc light as she heard them coming above them, their deathly payload dropping across the city. Finding one, she stuck to it as long as she could, the guns finding it. Smoke suggested it was hit and she hoped she'd downed it.

They were moving away, but they were coming back for another round. Dory tried to find them, but the sound was retreating.

Fire lit up the skyline against the luminous orange and red glows. The searchlight traveling across the sky, searching for the direction they would come from.

"Southwest," Vera said, training her binoculars again. Directives were fed through her headphones from the listening posts outside the city. Dory quickly wound the light around, accidentally brushing her elbow against the burning barrel of the light. She didn't know exactly how hot it was, but she could fry an egg on it.

The drone started in the distance and the guns started firing. That awful sound of the engines coming closer was the fiercest dread Dory had ever known, except perhaps when an awful man had tried to throw her over the side of a ship. That had been pretty awful too, but justice had eventually found that villain.

It didn't feel like justice was coming to these horrid Germans who were coming to devastate the city night after night. Dory had lost count how many nights, but they were relentless. If only there would be a clear night tomorrow so they could have a reprieve.

Bombs were dropping again, cutting sways across the city with glittering explosions. East London was where they focused, hoping to hit the docks. They followed the River Thames until they reached London.

"More coming from the east," Vera called, and Dory used all her strength to quickly wind the light around, the light traveling along the clouds. This second squadron was coming in just as the first was retreating. Dory knew it was going to be a heavy night.

Fire dotted across the city, creating a red glow on the clouds above, interspersed by curtains of glowing smoke. One trace of whistling didn't seem to end, it just grew louder and louder. A painful twist in her heart told Dory that this one was going to be close. Thunder shook the building under their feet and Dory bumped her elbow into the side of the lamp again. The second fell, perhaps a street further away. The impact of it reverberated through her body.

"That was close," Vera said. "I hope the people in the India Docks shelter are okay."

Feeling shaken, Dory returned her hands to the wheel that turned the light. Now was not the time to think about how close that had been. She had a job to do. Still, it was a thought she couldn't entirely push away. Night after night up on this roof, they wondered if this was the night they would be struck. They were seen after all. The searchlights were the most visible part and some of the planes seemed to aim for them.

Down the street, fire had broken out and they could see the outlines of the windows of the façade—hear the rumble of a building collapsing. "That was more than an incendiary," Dory said.

The peppering of the bofor guns continued, relentlessly searching for a target, and the drone returned. Dory found another plane and stayed with it until the guns found it. They were hard to take down. The Germans built their planes well and it usually took a period of sustained firing to bring one down. Sometimes they did crash into the city, turning into bombs themselves.

The yell of the firemen could be heard as they raced up the street to quell the nearby fire. A new wave of planes was approaching, and Dory forgot about the firemen and turned her attention to finding a new target, but they were flying further away and the sounds of the bombs hitting were more muffled.

"Do you think they're targeting more westwards?" Betsy asked from the door.

It did seem that way. "Maybe they're trying to hit Parliament," Dory replied.

"Sounds awful, but it would be good if it wasn't us all the time."

Betsy was a local girl, having grown up just a few streets back from the dock, in a neighborhood that seemed to get the bulk of the Germans' attention as they were trying to destroy the industrial heart of the country. Around here was where all the factories were, where the docks and storehouses were. Hitting Parliament and St Paul's would be symbolic victories and would serve little to slow down the British war effort. No doubt the German spies would know exactly where the Ministry of War was located, but from what Dory gathered, it was a ministry that was very good at contingency planning. Livinia worked there, of course, but wouldn't be there at night—instead safe somewhere in the West End.

"I think they're retreating," Betsy said. "The radar says they are moving away."

"They did enough damage," Dory said, continuing to search until the all-clear sounded.

This was the moment when it felt as though the entire city was listening, and all that could be heard were the fires, sometimes screams.

They seem to have gone. Dory searched, her light traveling across the sky. It took a good ten minutes before the all-clear sounded and the blaring tone of the sirens broke out across the city.

"I hope that is it for tonight," Vera said.

"I hope so too. I think the carbon needs to be changed." Dory knew her light well enough to tell when the carbon was weakening. She would have to change it in the morning when it had cooled down.

Light rain sizzled on the lamp and was turning into steam. Rain would help quell the fires, but it was only light drizzle at this point.

The yell of the fire and rescue men continued down the road. People would be emerging from their shelters all over the city, walking home by the light of numerous fires.

It could well be that the Germans came back. They had before and the sirens would fire up, calling everyone back into the shelter.

Her light was weakening further. "I might turn it off. The carbon is going."

Turning the switch, Dory turned off the light, plunging them into darkness. For a moment, not even the fires of the city were visible to them until their eyes adjusted.

Walking over the edge of the roof, Dory sat down. Half of her body was burning hot, the rain soothing on her red cheek. Taking off her helmet, she let the rain cool her head as she brought out a sandwich. She was starving hungry. They would wait here until dawn in case the enemy returned for another go.

Betsy still wore her headphones which fed her directions. Betsy sat downstairs, manning the large radio and the electrical supply for the searchlight. The whole top story of the building was taken over to support the searchlight.

A thin slice of ham gave her sandwich barely more than flavor. She ached for some vegetables and remembered the lovely tomatoes they had grown at Lady Pettifer's villa in the south of France. Such abundance seemed so far away now, almost unbelievable.

"I thought I would go dancing tomorrow if it's a clear night. They suggest it might be clear." Vera had a scheduled evening off and was seeing a man who worked on the Watch.

"That would be nice," Dory said. Dancing wasn't something Dory loved as much as Vera. For her it wasn't easy having a good time, when so many were fighting across the Channel, but those same men came home for a few days and wanted to do little else but have a good time. Even with all the bombs dropping, they still managed.

Chapter 3

THERE WAS SMOKE in the air when Dory walked home at dawn. The rescue brigade was still out, quelling fires and searching through the rubble.

The streets were full of people returning to their houses. Most slept in the air raid shelter, or tried to. Returning to their houses at the break of dawn to carry on with their day.

Dory was heading for bed. It had been a long night and working the searchlight, with all the energy and anxiousness expended, she was utterly drained. It seemed her body ran on anxiousness these days. Even in her sleep, it couldn't be assured that bombs wouldn't start dropping. They tended not to anymore during the day, but it could still happen. Or worse, dreaded news that the Germans were crossing the channel to invade. Anything could happen while she slept.

A woman was putting an 'Open for Business' sign on a store where the windows had all been shattered. Intact windows were a luxury these days. So far, they still had theirs on the terrace house she shared with Vera and Betsy. A typical two rooms upstairs, two downstairs. With so many people homeless, they were thankful for having a roof over their heads.

Walking down Pennyfield Street, smoke grew thicker and the rescue brigade had lorries and ambulances along the street. This must be where one of the bombs dropped. It was probably the one Dory had seen during the night.

Glass crunched under her feet as she walked, staying on the other side of the street from where all the activity was, but she couldn't avoid seeing the bodies of four people laying on stretchers. Obviously someone had built their own air shelter at home, but it hadn't been enough for a direct hit. There weren't enough air shelters for everyone. It had been a bone of contention in the community and the Government had sent out pamphlets advising people how they could build one at home.

It hadn't served these people, though.

One of the bodies was a child and Dory felt her heart twist, unable to bring herself to look away. The body was so covered in dust, it looked almost indistinguishable from the rubble it had been drawn from. With so much dust, they must be hard to find.

The Government didn't release information about the people who died in the bombings. Nothing regarding the numbers of dead was printed in the newspapers—only the location of strikes. But they were so abundant, they were often not reported anymore. Information of any kind was hard to get these days. One had to inquire about someone specifically to get an answer.

"Move along," a police officer said, waving her along the road.

With a tight smile, Dory continued, but quickly looked back. The second body was a woman, and then two men. One of them wore green corduroy pants and a woolen vest. Brown shoes.

Tearing her gaze away, she continued walking. A mobile tea bus stood at the end of the road, and Dory fished through her pockets for two shillings. A warm cup would perhaps revive her a little.

"It's awful, isn't it?" the woman with blond curls said as Dory approached the small window at the side of the bus and asked for a tea with milk. Sugar wasn't an option anymore. What Dory wouldn't give for a bit of jam or a piece of chocolate. Still, the condensed milk did add some sweetness. "They were in their house, too."

"Yes, I saw it last night."

"You're one of the ATS girls."

"Yes," Dory confirmed. "On the searchlight down the road."

"Ah. I was in the Dee Street shelter myself. We all felt it. Poor Sandra, and her child too." The woman tsked with sadness.

"You knew them?"

"Well, you do, don't you? I'm stationed here every day. They came down to buy a tea both her and her husband. He was quite partial to a Chelsea Bun on a Friday. Worked in the sail factory down the road."

"Who was the other man?"

"What other man?"

"There were two men pulled out of the rubble."

"They must have had a visitor. As far as I know, no one else lived with them. Oh, it's so awful." The woman shuddered and then had to serve a customer.

Blowing on the hot tea in a chipped enamel cup, Dory moved away, finally taking a swallow of the hot liquid. It warmed her insides and she sat down on a low brick wall to finish it. Lorries trundled past and merchants set up shop. Children ran along the street, getting themselves off to school.

Dory didn't have enough money to buy a bun, but there was a bit of bread and cheese waiting for her at home, a snack before bedtime.

Finishing her tea, she returned the empty cup and quickly wiped the dust off her backside before continuing home. Tiredness was dogging her steps, which grew heavier the closer she got to her bed, but as she turned down her own street, she saw a crater in the middle of the road. Their street had been struck and there was now a substantial hole in it. Well, cars wouldn't be coming through here anytime soon.

With a vice of dread around her heart, she continued home, to find that the bomb had knocked over the tree in their garden. A flurry of branches and leaves, but Dory could also see that it had taken out part of their kitchen wall. The window on the upper story was also shattered—more from the impact of the bomb than from the tree. Scorch marks scarred the stucco wall that still stood.

"Just wonderful," Dory said and walked around the tree to the door. She had to use her elbow to get it open, the wall having shifted slightly. Inside the kitchen, every surface was covered in dust and bricks were strewn across the floor. Not to mention the treetop now decorating the whole side of the kitchen. Well, the stove was intact, but Dory doubted the electricity was.

Testing the light, she confirmed that the electricity had been taken out. It would be ages before they could get someone to reattach it. Still, they were lucky. They still had a roof and three walls. Better than some had it. There was nowhere for people to go when they lost their houses to a bomb. Often they simply wandered during the day, and stayed in the air shelters at night. Not much else you could do when your home was turned into a pile of rubble.

Wiping the dust off the bench with her hand, she opened the bread tin and pulled out the loaf to cut herself two slices. The water still worked, she noted. At least the bomb hadn't hit the water main.

While eating her cheese sandwich, Dory started picking up the bricks from the floor and carrying them out into the front yard. They would have to find a saw to cut branches off the tree. The trunk would likely have to stay where it was for the time being. Perhaps someone would find a use for it and carry it away. Nothing went to waste. They had to save absolutely everything from rags to bones left over from supper. Apparently they all had a use somewhere.

"Hells bells," Vera said as she walked through the door. "I said I liked outdoor dining, but this is a bit far."

"Who do you think we can call to take the tree trunk away?"

"I don't know," Vera said. "I'll ask Kevin." Kevin was her boyfriend and warden in the area. "Has Betsy seen it?"

"No, she said she needed to go to her mothers."

Betsy was a local girl, while Vera came from Liverpool.

"She's not going to be happy," Vera continued. "Did you see the window was blown out?"

"Yes," Dory said. Her room was in the back, so most likely, her window was still intact. It was the smaller of the rooms, so she had it to herself, while Vera and Betsy shared the larger room at the front of the house. "We will have to find a pane somewhere. Do you think Kevin can help?"

"I'll have him go to the salvage yard, but glass is hard to come by. We might have to board it up. Let's finish cleaning this up once we've had some sleep."

Dory could only agree. This all felt additionally desolate because she was so tired, so she stopped and closed the front door inside it's warped frame. "Hopefully the house won't fall down."

"It should be alright," Vera said. "Or we might be showing more of our private business to the whole street. Could you imagine if the wall fell away while we slept? I am so tired, I probably wouldn't notice. There's going to be glass all over my bed." It was unlikely the house would fall down as this was a terrace house and the structural walls were between the houses.

"Do you want some help?"

"No, I'll manage," Vera said with a smile. "Let's sleep and deal with it later."

Retreating to her little room, Dory pulled off her jacket and hung it up, then her dark green trousers, to slip into her welcoming bed. Sleep took her almost immediately, but she did register Betsy's swearing when she came home.

Chapter 4

THE MESS SEEMED even worse when Dory woke. Vera was already cleaning up and there were men outside, contemplating the sizeable hole in the road.

"I borrowed a saw from Harriet," Vera said, pointing to a rusty saw lying on the table. "I thought we should at least get rid of the branches."

"Some would say it's a nice look," Dory replied, grabbing the saw. "In some circles, having a tree inside is all the rage."

"Perhaps a nice decorative palm, not a great, big ash tree through the side of the wall."

Starting at where the wall used to be, Dory started sawing the branches of the tree.

"What's the weather like?" Vera asked.

"Cloudy. I doubt it will be a clear night." Everyone prayed for a clear night. The bombers didn't come.

They still had to man the searchlights, but would merely be sitting there on the roof drinking tea, and everyone in the city would be safe that night. Unfortunately, there had been very few clear nights of late. A reprieve would do the whole city a world of good, but it didn't look like it.

"If you keep going with the branches, I'll fry us a couple of eggs."

Hunger gnawed at Dory's stomach, but it was a feeling she was getting used to. They weren't starving, but there was never quite enough.

"Post," a man called from outside.

"Hello, Howie," Vera said. "How is everything?"

"Can't complain. Many have it worse," the older man in his late sixties said. He'd been retired before the war started, but as all the young men had left, he'd been asked into service again. "We keep ticking on, don't we? Two letters today. I see your tree wanted to come in. Didn't like it outside anymore?"

"Who does?" Vera said and accepted the small bunch of letters. "See you tomorrow, Howie."

"Right then," he said with a tap to his cap.

"Letter for you," Vera said and handed a white envelope to Dory.

Dory expected a letter from Lady Pettifer, but it wasn't her handwriting. Staring at it for a moment, she knew it was from DI Ridley, or Captain Ridley, as he was now called. It was the first time in a long time that he had written and Dory didn't know what to do. Should she rip it open and read it right now, or save it for later? She decided on the latter, tucking it away in her pocket.

There would be no end of questions from Vera and Betsy if they knew a man was writing to her, and also, she wanted to read it when she was ready.

Having cleaned the dust off the frying pan, Vera was starting to fry a couple of eggs for them. They had run out of ham and wouldn't be getting any more until next week. They weren't the most frugal—unable to make their rations last a whole week. They were out of lard too, which made the eggs hard to peel off in one piece.

"I think we should go to the hall for dinner before work tonight," Vera said.

"Sure."

The hall was a standard restaurant, which had cheap, basic meals. Without children or families, the wage provided by the ATS was sufficient to provide a few extras, and the restaurants were good for when rations had run out.

Returning to the work at hand, Dory continued cutting through the branches, while Vera turned on the radio. There was a play on, interrupted by public service announcements urging them to do without. They even sang it in a jingle, '*If in doubt, do without.*'

"I am so tired of being told what to do every moment of the day. It's as though they believe we are completely incapable of thinking for ourselves," Betsy said, appearing at the door. The impressions of her pillow were still pressed into her cheek. "Save this, save that. Don't be greedy. We have nothing to be bloody greedy with, do we?"

"Good morning, sunshine," Vera said.

"And that bloody hole in the road. The clog heads have been out there talking about what to do about it the whole morning. Fill the damned thing. Why is that so hard? It's not like there's a shortage of rubble. And what about our wall?"

"I doubt anyone is going to worry about the wall. Well, we're lucky no one got hurt."

"There's going to be people in here pilfering our clothes the minute we leave tonight." Betsy grumbled as she sat down. "Maybe I can ask Harriet to stay the night. They're stepping on each other's toes every moment of the day over there."

"I don't mind," Dory said. "She can sleep in my room."

"Our house is going to turn into a flophouse," Betsy said.

"Maybe for the best until we work out how to sort the wall," Vera said.

"Or we just lock the door to the kitchen," Dory said.

"We haven't got a key to that lock."

That was a point. "I got the key to my room. Perhaps we should swap the locks."

"Well, I will leave that up to you," Betsy said, finally cheered when receiving a plate of egg on toast from Vera.

Locksmithing wasn't a skill Dory had, but tradesmen were near on impossible to find. How hard could it be to change out a lock? It would be something she would worry about after her breakfast. They only had a few hours before it was time to head off to work.

"Still, we are lucky no one was hurt," Vera said as she brought over two more plates to the table.

"They weren't so lucky on Pennyfield Street," Dory said. "The family was at home."

"It's heartbreaking when they drag them out of the rubble."

Involuntarily, Dory's mind returned to the sight—the young girl covered head to toe in dust. Then the man with the green corduroy trousers. He wasn't covered in dust. "Are they always covered in dust?"

"Any I have seen," Vera said. "A house goes down and it more or less pulverizes."

Cutting into the egg, the yolk bled bright yellow, like liquid sunlight.

*

After replacing the carbon filament and cleaning the mirrors, Dory took a moment to return downstairs to the operations room for their searchlight station. There was no indication of the Luftwaffe coming just yet. Betsy was out the back, tinkering with the radio—something about the transistor. Dory had no idea how a radio worked.

Taking a seat at the desk, she turned on the desk light and brought out the letter she had been saving all day.

The envelope was battered but intact. It had a black stamp on it that said 'Field Post Office' and another in blue that said 'Passed by Censor.' Ridley's handwriting was neat and crisp, stating her name and address. There was no return address, but she still wrote to him on the base at Pirbright. It seemed to get through eventually. How long it took to reach him, she had no idea.

With a penknife, she slid along the top of the envelope, the cutting sounding harsh. The paper was thin, folded three times. It had only a few lines, and it looked as though he'd been in a hurry. It was postmarked only a few days ago, so his letters traveled quickly.

Dear Miss Sparks, it started. He rarely called her Dory.

I hope I find you well. I travel a great deal more as the war progresses, and I can tell you very little about what I am doing. I shall be back in London at the end of the month. Unfortunately only for a few days. Perhaps I could call on you then.

Dory blinked, surprised that he wanted to call on her, and nervous at the thought already. Over time, she got increasingly nervous seeing him, and distracted by thoughts of him.

She had written to him when she'd first moved to London, informing him of her change in circumstances.

I hear of the nightly bombings and am distressed to think that you face them every night. Be safe.

Regards,

M. Ridley

Dory read the letter over and over again, trying to glean any new understanding out of them. It warmed her heart thinking he worried about her. No doubt what he was up to would terrify her. People in military intelligence were supposedly exactly where they weren't supposed to be, but they were absolutely tight-lipped about what they got up to. Perhaps it was best she didn't know, or she would lie awake and worry endlessly as she lay in bed.

The idea of him not returning from the war was the worst thought she could conceive of. Her brother was still too young to serve, but if this war stretched on, it would absorb him as well. Hopefully the people on the radio saying this war would be over by spring were right.

Seeing him in a few weeks would cheer her. He felt so distant. Not that she had any claim on him in any way. They had never been romantically involved. Had never even shared a meal together, except that one time in a pub near Wallisford Hall, but she had barely known him then.

Chapter 5

THE USUAL MAYHEM was inflicted upon the city. It was so strange to consider this usual, but it was. Death falling from the sky had become commonplace. If at all possible, it was best not to think about it. Come dawn, life went on. Not for everybody, though.

Unwillingly, Dory's thoughts returned to the family. It was so awful the child was there, but Dory knew that many hadn't sent their children away somewhere out in the country. If they would have done so, the girl would still be alive—albeit alone and an orphan.

There just weren't any upsides to any of this. It was just awful.

Something really bothered her, though and she couldn't put her finger on why. There was a niggle in the back of her mind that refused to budge—or reveal what the problem was. But she'd had this feeling before. Something was wrong—off, somehow.

The Gentleman on Pennyfield Street

Pennyfield Street was on her way home and she walked down it, seeing the pile of rubble that had once been the inflicted house. No one was there searching through the rubble anymore. It was deserted now, another ghost of a building. Glass still crunched under her feet, but there was glass all over the city now.

A woman was standing with her arms crossed on the opposing side of the street, staring at the rubble. She wore a flowered dress and her hair was covered by a shawl. Her windows had been blown out like many of the others on the street.

"I had one fall on my street too," Dory said. "Middle of the street though. Sent a tree through my kitchen wall."

"Few streets don't have one or two. Don't know what we're to find in the mornings as we crawl out of the earth like moles. If they'd just gone to the shelter, they would be breathing today. Had problems with her nerves that woman. Why I reckon they stayed in their house." The woman clearly didn't approve of her neighbor. "Still, can't wish that on anyone. Little Madga there and all. I saw them pull 'em out."

"And the guest. I understand they had a guest."

"They never had guests. Kept to themselves those two. He'd have a pint at the pub every once in a while, but never one for socializing. So if you tell me they had a guest, I won't believe it. Don't know who that man was; I've never seen him before."

Dory frowned. She would have assumed it was an uncle or something. "He was an elderly man from what I saw."

"Bodies turn up everywhere, don't they?" the woman said and turned around to pick up her broom and start sweeping around the tinkling glass. "Who knows if there'll be anyone left standing once those Germans are done."

With a nod, Dory kept walking. Maybe the man had simply been someone passing by who needed to find shelter, but why hadn't he gone to a proper shelter. It could still be that he was a visito the neighbors had never seen before. It certainly wasn't out of the realm of possibility.

Still, something really bothered her, even as she tried to put it out of her mind. There was a reply letter to write to Captain Ridley. In a way, she had no idea what to say. Would he want to know about the hardship they had back here? Unlikely. The material distributed by the Ministry of Information suggested it was their duty to keep up the spirits of the fighting men. That they didn't need to know that their families were being bombed to smithereens back home.

Then there was the whole affair about Ridley returning to London that set butterflies flaring in her stomach. Would he actually want to see her? He had indicated so. They weren't officially anything to each other, so it was hard to know what to think—or what to write.

That man hadn't been covered in dust like the other bodies dragged out of the house on Pennyfield Street. How could that be? Had he simply happened to be protected from the dust—as if wrapped in a curtain? Was that even a possibility?

Her frown followed her all the way home, where Kevin was out in the yard, furiously sawing at the branches of the tree. His jacket was draped over the fence and Vera carried the branches out to the mortar wall.

"Won't have to use the door at all soon. We can simply walk straight into the kitchen," Vera said, checking her perfectly curled light brown hair in her small pocket mirror. "You took your time."

"I guess I walked slowly."

As per usual, Betsy had gone to see her mother, who worried about them being up there on that roof every night, facing the Germans head-on.

"Kevin, may I ask? The bodies that are pulled out of fallen buildings, are they always covered in dust."

"More or less. Sometimes they're completely charred."

That was not the answer she was looking for. "So if someone was pulled out relatively clean."

"Not even the live ones come out clean," he said, setting to task on another branch.

Dory didn't press, getting the feeling she wasn't going to get the answer she sought. Or maybe she had the answer she sought and it didn't make sense. "I'm gonna go up and rest," she said instead and Vera smiled at her.

"You look tired. You're not getting gloomy, are you? I think you need a night of dancing."

The last thing she wanted was a night of dancing with over-eager strangers. What she wanted was to know why this man had been pulled out of the rubble looking like a collapsing building didn't leave a mark on him. Other than blood. There had been blood on his face and forehead. She only just recalled this.

The letter to Ridley would have to wait until that afternoon. Right now, too much was weighing on her mind. Shutting herself away in her room, she poured water into her washing bowl and wiped her down her arms and face. Using the rag, she wiped her hair as well. There was so much dust in the city. Every wind gust picked it up and spread it across the entire city. At times, it felt as if they would never be clean again.

"Mail," Betsy said at the door and Dory went to open it. It was a light blue envelope, which meant it was from Lady Pettifer.

"Thanks," Dory said and closed the door again, ripping the top open with her finger as she lay down on the bed and crossed her ankles. A five-pound note was included, which was completely unnecessary, but Lady Pettifer did insist on giving her money every now and again.

Dear Dory,

I figured you could use this. I tried to send you some jam, but the postman wouldn't take it, completely getting above himself, the odious man. I hope to find you well. We are drowning in chickens here. A troop full of girls have come to manage them all. Sweet girls, who have set up their quarters in the stables. We don't need them now as the army commandeered all our horses. Poor things. My brother's horses are too temperamental for warfare, but they wouldn't listen.

I do hope you will come see me when you can. We haven't seen Livinia nor Vivian for a good while. My brother worries about both of them, especially Vivian who is in France. Livinia is being overseen by Lord Corrington, so that gives some assurance. He is a sensible man and will ensure she doesn't do anything unwise. We worry about Vivian, though. By far unsuited for war, I say, but no one listens to me. He has been promoted as captain, I understand, although he says nothing about where he is or what he is doing. The boy was never good at writing. Always too caught up with his own life to assure the people who worry for him.

We read of the nightly bombings and I do worry for you, too. The things you must see. If only this wretched war would end.

Yours Sincerely,

Lady Constance Pettifer

It was strange to think Vivian was now the same rank as Ridley. They were such different men. Ridley with his seriousness and competence, and Vivian being the exact opposite. She and Vivian had had a contentious relationship since the moment they'd met. He never quite approved of her—her presence or even more generally.

The last she had seen him, he'd gone to rescue his notorious mother from a sanitorium in Switzerland as the Nazis were skirting the borders. Lady Wallisford was apparently ensconced in the Bahamas, or was it Bermuda? Exiled, but never truly facing justice for murdering poor Nora Sands.

Dory wondered if she should tell Lady Pettifer about Ridley's letter and him mentioning that he might call on her when he returned to London. The lady respected the man and would likely be happy with this development, but then she would probably assume things were there that weren't. No doubt, she would be planning their wedding at the mere mention that he wrote to her.

Chapter 6

FEELING GROGGY, Dory opened her eyes and saw the sunshine streaming through the window. It was a nice day, it turned out. Maybe even a warm late autumn day. That would be nice for a change. Just a moment to sit in the sun. It sounded heavenly.

Then other thoughts encroached. The man in Pennyfield Street. Something was still very wrong and she couldn't simply ignore it. The Ministry of Information's publications kept saying one needed to keep watch and report anything that was out of the ordinary. What and to whom, though?

Could she go to the constabulary and say something? There was nothing to report though, other than that she had a bad feeling about this body. They would dismiss her without second thought. The insistence that he should be more dusty was probably not of much interest, especially as they didn't know who he was or why he was there. Just some man who turned out to be less dusty than he should be. Hardly damning evidence that something might be wrong.

Perhaps she could lay this at ease if she could find out who the man was. For all she knew, they knew exactly who he was, even if the neighbor hadn't. He could very well have had his papers in his pocket and his presence in Pennyfield Street made perfect sense.

Still, feeling a bit groggy, which she tended to when she woke up in the afternoon, she made her way downstairs where Betsy was sitting by the kitchen table, the hole in the wall more noticeable now that the tree branches were cut back.

"Morning," Betsy said. "There's a fried egg in the pan if you want it."

"Lovely," Dory said and walked over to take the bread out of the tin.

"What about this sun? We might have a clear night tonight."

"Let's hope so."

"This weather will do our tomatoes good." None of them were terribly good gardeners. Their plants only managed to produce one or two vegetables before consistently dying off. They didn't thrive in the soil and none of them could determine why. Poplar wasn't filled with skilled gardeners, although Lady Pettifer could probably determine what the soil needed.

With the spatula, Dory placed the fried egg on top of her bread slice, her stomach rumbling with the smell of food. As she sat down at the table, Betsy finished her meal. "As I recall, you know someone who works in the rescue brigade."

"Frank Waters. He lives just down the road at thirty-eight. Nice bloke. Not sure why they wouldn't accept him into the forces. He's kept that quiet. Why do you ask?"

"Something is bothering me about that house on Pennyfield Street."

"Something always bothers you. You have the most suspicious mind. Nefarious plots everywhere."

"I do not," Dory said, surprised that Betsy would say such a thing.

"Weren't you saying you chased down some murderer in France?"

"I said a body was found at a party I went to. And maybe I did make some inquiries about it, but I don't suspect plots everywhere."

"Really, so you don't expect something untoward at that house in Pennyfield?"

That was hard to argue, because something was off about that man being there. "I'm just curious."

"Curiosity killed the cat."

"Nonsense. I have never seen a cat killed by curiosity. Motorcars mostly." Dory felt a little put out by the accusation. How could she be blamed for noticing strange things? But then Betsy had been a little snippy ever since Dory had mentioned her life in France, accusing her of having high and mighty associations. That little look of disapproval appeared every time a letter arrived from Lady Pettifer. "Technically, I think most of them die of old age."

After taking her plate to the sink, Betsy left, leaving Dory to stare out at the street, where Mrs. Mellison from next door waved at her through the hole. "Lovely weather today," she said.

Dory smiled and waved back, not exactly thrilled that the whole street could see them having their meals, but compared to many, they were lucky to have a roof over their heads and most of their walls.

Finishing her breakfast, she placed the plate in the sink and left the house in search of Frank Waters. Down the street at number thirty-eight, a woman was sweeping dust out of the front door. Looking up, she gave an absent smile.

"Is this where Frank Waters lives?"

"What do you want with my Frank?"

"I was hoping he could answer some questions for me about his work."

"I suppose you can catch him in the back shining his shoes. Best to go around. There's a gate around the corner"

Following the directions, she found a gate and reached through the hole to the locking mechanism. A man was sitting on a chair in his white undershirt, his suspenders undone at his sides. "Mr. Waters?" Dory asked.

"Who's asking?" he said gruffly. Dory could see he would be good at rescue, being a strong and muscular man. It was surprising he hadn't been accepted into the forces. Physically there looked nothing wrong with him. A cigarette sat between his lips and bobbed up and down as he spoke.

"Dory Sparks. I'm one of the ATS girls. I was hoping to find someone who worked on that collapsed building on Pennyfield Street."

Putting his boot down, he leaned back and considered her. "Four bodies. What concern is it of yours?"

"I was curious about the man you pulled out. When I happened to speak to the neighbor, she couldn't account for who he was, and said they never had visitors."

"Where are you from? Posh accent if I ever heard one."

Apparently he had never heard one, because hers was nowhere near posh. "Not really. I'm from Swanley."

"Went there once."

"So about this man. Do you know if he was identified?"

"We don't identify them, only pull them out."

"Then who does?"

"That would be the morgue."

"And where was he taken?"

"Royal London, I think. Most of them get taken there. A few to the Tower. Most people don't know they have a morgue there. Where all the river floaters get taken. On a bad night, the Royal gets full and we have to go to the Tower with the spillover."

More information than Dory needed to know. She'd never heard anyone speak so casually about bodies, but supposed it was something you became desensitized to if you dealt with them all day. "I see," she said. There was something unnerving about this man and his great, powerful hands, seemingly strangling the little shoe polishing cloth.

"As I passed, I noticed he hadn't much dust on him. Is that usual?"

"Nosy one, aren't you?"

Keep focus on the question rather than me, she wanted to say, but she only smiled, hoping the silence would urge him to speak. "It's not normal," he finally said. "Normally they're beige from head to toe. Not a scrap of skin or color seen on them. Bloody messes most of the time. Gets everywhere that dust. So does the blood. You can't really see the blood until you touch it. Covered in dust too, but it sticks like glue when you have it on you."

Dory could imagine that woman sweeping inside having to wash that out of his clothes on a daily basis. At least the carbon rubbing off the filaments were easy to wash out. "Thank you for your time," she said. "I won't disturb you further."

His reply was only a grumble, but she caught the word 'hoity' in there. Some in this part of London were not all that welcoming to people who didn't grow up here. On the whole, they were the most friendly, generous people one could meet, but not all of them. Frank Waters left her with a distinct wariness and she was glad to be away from him. Maybe the armed forces had denied him because of sheer uneasiness.

At least she had a second opinion telling her that it was unusual for a body to be so clean. At this point, she hadn't asked herself what she thought that meant. From what she could see, it could only be that he hadn't been in the house when it had fallen down, but at this point, she had little faith in her own deliberations. She was, by far, not an expert on these things.

For a moment, she wondered if she should write to DI Ridley—Captain Ridley, she reminded herself—but maybe she should mention all this to Lady Pettifer.

If people thought her curious, they hadn't met Lady Pettifer, who loved going over every detail. Dory would write her that night if indeed it stayed clear. For now, though, she might walk over to the Royal London Hospital to inquire about the body. Perhaps the mystery had been cleared up already.

Chapter 7

AN EXPANSE OF YELLOWISH brick stretched before Dory as she stared up at the Royal London Hospital. A clock at the center told her she only had an hour before she needed to head off. Even on a clear day, they had to be ready in case it clouded over and the Luftwaffe followed.

A man knocked into her in his rush to get into the hospital, not even turning to apologize. It seemed everyone was in a hurry. Dory followed the man who had disappeared from sight into a hall leading to a landing with a jumble of metal staircases. All the walls were painted white. Everyone was in a hurry, except the people sitting around in wheelchairs with one part or another bandaged.

Most of the people here couldn't get home, she realized, or had no home to go to. Still, they were the lucky ones.

"Excuse me," she said to a harried-looking nurse in her white uniform. Her nurses cap turned as her head did, and she checked the small timepiece pinned to her chest. "I'm seeking the morgue."

"Through those doors on the left and down the stairs, as far as they'll go. Then left and another right." Before saying anything more, she was gone and Dory was left to wonder which of the two sets of doors on the left she meant. Well, at least it narrowed it down to two.

Dory picked the door on the immediate left and was met with an unpleasant chemical smell. There were beds in the corridor with patients. Most were quiet and Dory felt as if she was disturbing them by walking past. A mother hovered over a small lump in a bed, cooing and whispering.

A staircase came into view and she slipped down them, meeting a grieving pair in black. It seemed she was going to the right place. A sign for the morgue appeared at the bottom with a hand pointing to the right, leading to a dingy waiting room filled with people. Three people were working behind a desk with frantic efficiency.

"Delaney," one of them called and a pair came forward from the awaiting mass.

"Can I help you?" one of the nurses demanded.

"I am here about a body."

"Most are," she said.

"Found on Pennyfield Street two days back."

"Are you a relative?"

"No," Dory said. "I am investigating some inconsistencies."

The nurse turned her head, unimpressed.

"I'm with the ATS," Dory continued and produced her identification card. In no way was she supposed to use it in this way, but she knew she wasn't getting past this nurse otherwise.

"The ATS don't usually deal with bodies."

"As I said there have been some inconsistencies we need to clarify."

Giving Dory a narrow-eyed look, the nurse pulled over a heavy tome and looked through. "Day before yesterday, you said."

"No, the one before."

The woman turned a book leaf back. "There were four."

"It's one of the men I'm here about. The older gentleman."

"We have no identity registered."

"Are you able to identify him?"

"Not at this point."

The nurses gaze lingered. "I'll call Doctor Hannover to see if he can have a quick word with you. Take a seat."

With a smile, Dory retreated and looked up at the clock. She had fifty minutes until she needed to leave. Hopefully she could speak to this doctor before that.

Most of the people around her were grieving, or in shock. Some simply stared into space. One was telling off her children for fussing. Dory watched these relatives of the people killed. There were also other types that came and went behind the desk, clerical persons carting off armloads of paper apparently stacking up behind the desk.

Dory almost fell asleep in the cool, silent atmosphere. The only person talking was the woman on the phone behind the desk.

"Miss Sparks," a woman finally said and Dory's eyes flew open.

"Yes," she said and joined the woman.

"Come with me." She was led through a curved archway and almost bumped into a body lying under a sheet. "Mind your step."

It wasn't the only body lying in the corridor. The whole corridor was lined with bodies. And the room she walked past had bodies lying in rows all throughout the floor, not covered in sheets—covered in dirt and blood.

"We're struggling a bit with capacity," she called over the shoulder as if it was something she said to everyone. "In here."

Dory was shown into a room where most of the corpses were on tables, lying under sheets. The far wall was covered with doors polished almost to a mirror finish. A man stood with a bloodied apron, eating a sandwich. "Miss Sparks," he said, laying the sandwich down on a tray.

"I understand the ATS is interested in one of the bodies we have. A man in his sixties from Pennyfield Street. We have no identity for him."

"There have been some inconsistencies about his presence. I am trying to identify him."

"Well, you best hurry, we don't have room for the cadavers to hang around. Mr. Green Corduroys? When we don't have a name, we tend to use clothing or any distinguishing features." The man walked over to the wall of small doors and opened one, pulling the tray out.

There was the man, lying in his green trousers. A clipboard hung on the inside of the door. "No identification and the constable couldn't identify him."

"Is it not remarkable that he was pulled out of the building with so little dust on him?" Dory asked.

"Now that you mention it, it is unusual. Not so unusual if hit by shrapnel. Can happen even a hundred yards away from the actual explosion, but the ones that go down inside buildings are usually mincemeat." Dory winced at the expression. "Sorry, you form a black sense of humor working here."

"No doubt."

"Most of his injuries were about the head. Not usual. Not much about the body, which is also unusual, so I can perhaps concur that there are some inconsistencies. House coming down tends to do wretched thing to limbs, but his are all intact. If I didn't know better, I wouldn't have guessed he'd come out of a collapsed building. But sometimes they simply happened to be protected by something large like a wardrobe. Usual, but it can happen. Quite a few people hide in wardrobes. Usually the elderly. Rarely works out well against a bomb." He flipped the yellow paper on the clipboard. "No ID, no particular marks, nothing in his pockets. Well-fed appearance. Had an appendectomy. Quite recently. Unusual in a man that age. High mortality with appendicitis in the elderly, so he must have had a strong constitution, I would guess. Other than his fine sense of fashion, there is nothing more to say about him. Could have come from anywhere if no one in the neighborhood knew who he was. Happens quite often. You'd be surprised how many people are not where they should be when the bombs start dropping."

Doctor Hannover was certainly a chatty man. Seemed he took the opportunity when someone could listen.

With a bang, he rolled the tray back and shut the door. "Sorry, can't be of any more help."

"Thank you for your assistance, Dr. Hannover. I will hopefully return with an identity."

"When you find out, report it to the Imperial War Commission. They are keeping the records. Mr. Green Corduroys is scheduled to be transported to Brookwood tomorrow morning."

"I see," Dory said. "I don't think I will have an identity for him by then."

"Best of luck with your investigation," he said, returning to pick up his sandwich.

With a smile, Dory veered through the obstacle course of cadavers to exit the room, wishing herself out of there as soon as possible. It was the first time she had ever been inside a morgue and although it was interesting, she felt the unease traveling up her spine. Poor Mr. Green Corduroys. Or perhaps it was because she understood the body of Mr. Corduroy wasn't where it was supposed to be. In fact, he may not have been in the building at all when it collapsed, and placed there later. It was the perfect way of getting rid of a body. Obviously, not conclusive evidence, but it was a suspicious situation.

Even more so, it was curious that the man had nothing in his pockets. Who visits somewhere they shouldn't be without anything in their pockets? A key, at the very least, not to mention a wallet.

So the only things to go on were his clothes, which truly were not all that unusual. They spoke of a retired man with a modest budget for clothing. Hardly the height of fashion. Then there was the appendectomy. People had the appendixes out on a fairly regular basis, but there would be a record somewhere of it. Finding it might not prove possible, but it was the most solid lead she had.

Chapter 8

THE CLEAR NIGHT PLUNGED the temperature and Dory had to don her woolen fingerless gloves. The moon lit up the river and across the other bank. Jumping from one foot to the next, Dory tried to keep warm. For once they could see the barrage balloons above them, floating in the sky in whatever direction the wind blew them. They looked like small, dark spots in the sky.

The voices of people were heard down on the street, out for the evening in this apparent reprieve from the air raid shelters. A moment of freedom. Dory hoped it would last.

As for herself, she was putting off doing what she'd promised herself she would do: write a letter to Captain Ridley. Why she was putting it off, she had no idea? She just didn't know what to say. Everything she considered saying just sounded stupid. But equally, she hated being cowardly and this was nothing but sheer cowardice.

Vera sat in a chair and stretched her arms, yawning. Betsy was downstairs with the radio. They weren't needed, but they still had to be there. Things could change very quickly.

Grabbing the clipboard Dory had placed on the other chair, she walked over to the edge of the roof and crouched down to sit with her back against the wall. Pulling out the candle she had in her pocket, she lit it and put it down next to her.

"The wardens will have your hide for that candle," Vera said.

"Which is why I am hiding here in the corner. They'll never see it." It was strange how they were admonished for a small, insignificant light like a candle, when they manned the biggest light of all. Besides, there were no planes. Nothing was reported from the listening posts or radar stations along the coast. A little candle wasn't going to harm anyone, but the people enforcing the blackout where almost maniacal in their zeal, handing out fines to people lighting their cigarettes on the street.

Clipping the cream-colored piece of paper to the board, Dory stared at it. She still had lovely stationery left over from her days in St. Tropez. It would run out soon and she would have to resort to the tissue-thin writing paper that was available these days.

Dear Cpt Ridley, she started, but then didn't know how to proceed.

I am glad to hear you are well. We are here, as well, although there are fewer and fewer houses still standing with each night. The Germans are relentless and the colder temperatures aren't putting them off.

In a sense, she knew she was babbling.

Some are taking advantage of the conditions. Mostly people simply taking advantage, such as looting, but I fear it is also the opportunity for worse things amongst our dark streets and the general confusion. There has been some suggestion that a crime has been committed a street or so down from where I live, but as of yet, there is no identity of the man found.

Dory decided not to go into any further details on the subject of the body in Pennyfield Street. The truth was that the identity of the man might never be found, so he was simply a person that was missing, presumed dead.

"There's a red light at the end of the street," Betsy said, appearing on the roof. "I saw it out the window."

"What light?"

"There," Betsy said, walking to the edge of the building not far from where Dory was sitting. Blowing her candle out, Dory stood up and tried to see this red light. Lights of any kind were unusual—red lights even more so.

"That's the gas detector," Vera said with a gasp. "We're being gassed. Where's the gasmask?"

"It can't be," Dory said. "There's been no one dropping any bombs."

"That's what I thought," Betsy said.

"Doesn't mean we're not being gassed. There's Germans crawling all over the place for all we know. They could have just released it rather than drop it from a plane," Vera challenged.

"I don't smell anything," Dory said.

"I'm not putting that blemmin' gas mask on. It stinks."

The gas masks were uniquely unpleasant.

"It can be malfunctioning for all we know," Dory said. "It's the most likely conclusion under the circumstances."

"Maybe I better call it in," Betsy said. "If there's more than one going off around the city, then there might be a problem."

Betsy disappeared downstairs. There were so many people out and about that night. It would be the perfect time to release some chemical that choked people. There wasn't even the scent of anything unpleasant in the air, though. It had to be a malfunction. Still, fear gripped deep in her belly and it was only the sheer unpleasantness of the gas masks that kept her from pulling one on.

They were supposed to carry them everywhere. The war office feared the Germans using mustard gas on them, but so far, they hadn't, which was a mercy. It might be a much more unbearable war if they couldn't breathe the very air.

A shudder crept down Dory's spine.

"They say it's nothing to worry about," Betsy called and relief washed over Dory. At times, it felt as though she had no fear left in her—that she'd exhausted it all. When the bombs started falling, she had to focus on her task at hand or her thought would get lost in the horror that was happening out in the city.

As then, she felt the after-effects of fear on her body and she closed her eyes and tried to calm herself, remembering swimming in the warm Mediterranean Sea with its sparkling blue water. That usually did the trick. It was hard to imagine that was only mere months ago. It seemed like a lifetime.

Returning to her previous sitting position, she lit her candle again and reread what she'd written so far. She'd been on a roll for a while, but it had dried up now and she couldn't formulate a single thing to say.

It will be nice to see you when you arrive in London. Please keep well.

That would simply have to do. Unclipping the note, she tucked it away in her jacket to put in an envelope when she got home. It would be the job for the afternoon.

"They're coming!" Betsy yelled from downstairs. "Southwest. Ten minutes."

Whoever told Betsy, told the air raid wardens too, because seconds later, the whine of the sirens started, growing louder and louder. Yelling started down in the street as all the people who'd been enjoying a night out had to abandon their activities and find shelter.

Looking up at the sky, Dory could see that it was clouding over. The barrage balloons weren't as visible now. The Germans literally followed the cloud. They must have been waiting for it—maybe even circling until they could pounce. Dory didn't know the details of how they operated.

Dory turned on the lever that powered the light and it flickered before shining. The light grew in strength as the light warmed. It made a buzzing sound and it wouldn't take long for it to be too hot to touch.

The planes were heard in the distance, that awful droning sound. The other searchlights switched on across the river and further along, traveling across the sky. They weren't having a night of reprieve after all. And by the sounds of the drones, it was a large wave of planes. It was going to be a mess of a night.

The first bombs dropped over toward the western part of the city, which was unusual. Normally they focused exclusively on the east. The bombs went off with golden sparkles, lighting up the skyline, along with the hot slugs of the anti-aircraft fire. The red of the fires came later.

Dory quickly wound the searchlight in the direction the planes were coming from.

"Here we go," Vera said. "Round I've-still-lost-count."

The airplanes flew overhead, the sound of them almost reverberating down Dory's body, then the whistling sound of bombs dropping, and also the silent parachute mines. The falling ones hit first, scattering across the landscape behind them, then the second wave of bigger explosions from the parachutes.

"Bastards," Vera yelled.

Dory refused to look and continued to search for a plane to target. The guns across the river were firing relentlessly, but sadly, they did little damage to the enemy in comparison to what the enemy did to them. At this point, though, Dory had lost any moral squeamishness about targeting an enemy plane for destruction. If she could shoot them all down, she would.

Finding a target, she stuck to it until the guns joined her, a trail of smoke finally coming from the plane. It was grim satisfaction striking one. It wouldn't make it back across the Channel, and Dory didn't care what happened to it or the pilot. Ideally it wouldn't hurt anyone other than the crew coming down.

Maybe a hardness had developed in her, she wondered.

Chapter 9

THE SMOKE IN THE AIR was pervasive. It stung Dory's throat and got into both her hair and clothes. People were out trying to deal with the latest round of destruction wreaked upon the city. There was a bombed out building down one of the side-streets, it's bricks strewn across the entire road.

Through the jumble of lorries and vans, she saw dusty lumps laid down on the street, and sighed. More senseless deaths.

Right now, though, there was one particular death she was dwelling on. The edifice of the Royal London hospital peeked through the roofline in the distance. No billowing smoke, so it had fared intact through the night. It couldn't be taken for granted that any specific building would be there the next day. It gave the world a strange feeling of transience that she'd never experienced before.

She'd just mailed the letter to Captain Ridley, but neither of them might be there anymore by the time it arrived. It was difficult to think about, so she tried not to. One day at a time; it was the only way to get through this.

As before, the hospital was busy, patients being brought in and discharged, visitors coming and going, and the rush of staff dealing with a workload far beyond what this hospital was built for.

With a slight shudder, she walked past the corridor leading to the morgue. Hopefully, she would not end up lying on the floor down there like so many others.

"May I help you?" a woman said behind a tall desk.

"I'm seeking records," Dory said and again produced her ATS identification.

"You'll have to go across the street. They're not kept here. Number ninety-four."

Dory thanked the woman, but the nurse had already moved onto the next person, so Dory returned to the clear day outside with its constant smoke haze. The carefree days of summer seemed so far away, but then she hadn't been carefree for a long time. The last time was perhaps when she'd started working as a maid in Wallisford Hall, before she'd understood that the world would descend into such a mess. Looking back, they had all seemed so unaware. There had been talk of war, of course, but no one truly believed it would happen.

Unfortunately, the buildings across the road were not clearly labeled and Dory didn't know which to enter. None of them were particularly inviting, with doorways that gave little away.

A man was walking toward the nearest doorway. "Pardon me," Dory stated. "I am looking for number ninety-four."

"Two down," the man said and disappeared into the door.

"Two down which way?" Dory called, but he was gone.

A fifty percent chance either way, so Dory tried the left first, entering a building that didn't have the look or smell of a hospital at all. In fact, there seemed to be very few people in this building. The main entranceway contained a staircase and a series of wooden doors. There was nothing to indicate where she needed to go.

After a moment of hesitation, she knocked on one of the doors and peeked inside, seeing an office.

"Yes?" a man said, sitting at a desk, a cigarette lit in his hand.

"Records?"

"Down the hall," he said, pointing with his cigarette. "All the way down the back."

"Right," Dory said with a smile before following the directions leading through three sets of double doors. A nurse smiled tightly as she came the other way, looking very out of place in her white uniform in this building.

Finally she reached a last set of double doors, where small round windows were inlaid on each. Peering inside, she saw a man sitting at a desk. Behind him were stands with files. This had to be the place.

"Hello," Dory said as she walked in. The man with thinning hair looked up at her without smiling. "I need some assistance. This is the hospital records, I believe?"

"Yes," the man confirmed. "How may I assist you?"

"Well," she started with a smile, "I am trying to track a patient. At least I believe he was a patient here." It could have been another hospital in

London, or even elsewhere, but if he was a resident of the East End, which is an assumption she was starting her search with, then she this was where he would receive any medical treatment. "An elderly man who had an appendectomy not so long ago.

"Name?" the man asked.

"I don't have a name."

Now the man looked up. "How am I supposed to track him without a name?"

To this Dory didn't answer. "I realize it's not ideal."

"That's an understatement. Do you realize how many appendectomies are performed in this hospital every day?"

"I was led to believe they are less common with elderly gentlemen."

"Unfortunately, there is no way of searching for elderly men with appendectomies. Our records are not cataloged by age or even gender. They're cataloged by surname—which you don't have."

Dory wiped her fingers across the mouth, trying to think what to do. There was a good chance that somewhere in these records was the name of the man she was looking for—a veritable needle in a haystack. There would be a record of almost every person living and dead who lived in the area—except for her, as she had never been a patient here.

"Follow me," the man said and she did as he led her through a second set of doors, which led into complete darkness. The lever of a light sounded and hanging lights blinked on, revealing a warehouse-sized room with rows and rows of records.

A deep sigh escaped her as she realized what an insurmountable task it was to find it.

"There is some good news," the man continued. "Luckily, the information you seek is on the cards cataloging the system. Age, name and procedure, so you don't have to go through each file." He pointed over to a row of card drawers with small drawers labeled with gold letters. "There is a card for every person, probably close to a million—unless the person is deceased, for which the cards are taken out and placed in those sets of drawers over there, he said, pointing further down the side of the wall. "Is the person deceased?"

"Yes, but only recently and unidentified."

"I see. Then he should be in here somewhere. You can use the desk over there," he said and smiled tightly before leaving her.

With heavy steps, Dory walked over and sat down, turning on the small desk lamp. This wasn't an impossible task, but she would have to look through about a million cards of the people living in this area. She had no idea how long it would take. It could take weeks.

As she walked over to the first drawer with an 'A' stamped on it, she pulled out the long drawer. There were perhaps two or three thousand cards in this one drawer. Placing it down on the desk, she started rifling through it, looking for people born prior to 1880. The birthdate was written in the upper right corner, so it wasn't hard to see, flicking through each card. Anyone before, she then checked the name to see if they were male, thirdly if an appendectomy was listed in the procedures field within the last five years.

Going through the entire drawer, she hadn't found a single one. It had taken fifteen minutes to go through the drawer. For a moment, she wondered if she could perhaps speak directly to the surgeons to see if they recalled a case, but recognized that they did so many operations, it was unlikely they would recall the specific gentleman. Chances were she would end up back here anyway.

Returning the first set of drawers, she drew out another one and carried it back to the desk. It was too cold in here to take her jacket off, but her eyes grew adjusted to the poor lighting. At least the air wasn't full of smoke. It had that funny smell of paper that you sometimes got in bookshops or libraries, but much stronger.

After about a dozen drawers, she still didn't have a single name. Apparently appendectomies in the elderly were quite rare. Then she finally found one. A Mr. Findley of Whitechapel.

A serial number down the bottom referred to his full file and Dory went in search, but then wondered what she would gain by seeing his file. A noise disturbed her and she looked around the corner to see the records manager approaching. She'd forgotten his name, or hadn't gotten it at all.

"I have been considering your undertaking," he started as he approached. "It would perhaps be possible to look at the operation room rosters. They are recorded day by day, so there would be less to go through in total. In most cases, they do list the age and name of the patient, but not always. Not as accurate, but there is a good chance you might find something."

"Yes, please," Dory said. "I have only found one so far, and it's been three hours." She only had two more to look before she had to go to work for the evening.

"I'll retrieve them for you. How long back are you looking?"

"Five years."

"Return to the desk you were using and I will retrieve them."

Chapter 10

AS PROMISED, ON HER day off, she was going up to Wallisford Hall to visit Lady Pettifer. It had been a while since they'd seen each other, and Dory knew her friend was curious about her new life.

Anytime, she took the train up there, she seemed to get caught out for time and she'd found herself yet again running to catch her train.

The station was full of soldiers carrying their canvas bags, clearly happy to be home for a reprieve. A few were injured, with bandage slings holding arms up. Still, these were the lucky ones. No one had failed to see the young boys who had been engaged to deliver the dreadful telegrams with the worse news. Also dreadful was the fact that for many, you would never find out. If something happened to Captain Ridley, she wouldn't find out. Her letters would simply go unanswered.

Obviously, he had a mother somewhere, a family, but she didn't know enough about him in that regard. In reality, they knew very little about each other. She couldn't even remember if she'd even told him where she was from.

There was a stirring of guilt inside her for going to see Lady Pettifer on this rare day off instead of going to Swanley to see her mother. It was just that she had promised Lady Pettifer, and the older woman was more forthright in extracting promises.

Finding her train, Dory climbed onboard and took her seat. Lady Pettifer had sent her a first-class ticket, even though she didn't need Lady Pettifer to buy train tickets for her. It was perhaps a means of guaranteeing she would come.

The sights going north wasn't as terrible as those around the East End. There were bombed houses, but not to the degree the eastern parts of the city had, where whole blocks had been decimated. The city gave way to the countryside and Dory could pretend everything was normal. She had been such a different girl the first time she'd headed up to Wallisford Hall at barely nineteen years old.

On this visit, she would see her Aunt Gladys too, who still worked as a cook for Lord Wallisford. Because of that, though, her mother would soon find out about this visit, so Dory had better plan a trip home at the earliest opportunity.

The name placards had all been removed from the train stations, even within the towns they passed by. There were shops with village names covered or painted over. For what reason, Dory wondered? When she finally reached Quainton, the name had been removed there too and she was lucky she had come this way a few times before.

"Miss Sparks," said the vaguely familiar man who was the stationmaster.

"Yes," Dory said with a smile, embarrassed that she couldn't recall his name.

"I'm to run you up, just let me see this train off," he said. Moving down the platform to then lift his hand up and blow his whistle. The heavy train started chugging, gaining momentum with every turn of the wheels. Dory watched as the bellow of steam released along with the high-pitched whistle.

"This way," the man said and guided her to the exit. "I have my motorcar around the side of the building."

It was an older model black vehicle with beige leather seats. The engine whined when it started down the road. "Thank you so much for agreeing to drive me."

"Well, one doesn't agree so much as relent when it comes to Lady Pettifer," he said.

"That's true," Dory said with a smile. "Not much around here has changed."

"Not at first glance, perhaps, but all the young people are gone. It's just us older ones left."

It hadn't occurred to her that the stationmaster was driving her because there was no one to pick her up. Larry, who had collected her last time, would have been conscripted. Probably George as well.

Everything looked well, though. The stubble of the last harvest was still in the fields and everything looked perfectly normal as they turned into the long drive to Wallisford Hall. In truth, she hadn't believed she would ever come back here, but here she was.

The grand house that was Wallisford Hall was exactly the same, except Dory could see the chicken coops that Lady Pettifer had told her about in the distance.

"Thanks ever so much," she said to the stationmaster.

"Tell Lady Pettifer if she needs anything, she only has to ask," he said, tipping his hat and he set off, the wheels crunching along the gravel.

Dory walked around to the side of the house to find the kitchen entrance. "Woohoo," she said as she opened the door. "Gladys."

"Is that you, Dory?" she heard her aunt say as she hung her coat and hat up on the rack by the door. It looked disturbingly empty compared to how it had been before.

"I just got here. The stationmaster drove me."

"Nice man that Harry."

Glady's round form appeared with her arms outstretched. "Good to see you, pet," she said and embraced Dory. "Wasn't sure you'd ever come back when Lady Pettifer dragged you off to France."

"If it wasn't for this war, I'd probably still be there. Lovely place."

"I saw the postcards you sent."

"Where is everyone?"

"Ack. It's only me. Mrs. Parsons and Mr. Holmes now. Everyone else was called away. Three staff to manage this whole house; can you imagine? The garden is an absolute mayhem."

"Mavis and Clara too?"

"Clara is working on a farm up north, and Mavis in some factory somewhere. Building planes, I think. Not sure I would dare fly in a plane she'd built, mind you. Are you hungry?"

"I had a sandwich on the train."

"Come have some lemon drizzle cake."

"You have cake?" Dory said with astonishment.

"Only for special guests."

Dory blushed with delight. "I can't tell you how long it's been since I've had a slice of cake."

"I'll make you some tea. We'll have some before Lady Pettifer knows you're here."

"She might already know," Dory said, thinking of the stationmaster's motorcar.

"Well, family comes before others," Gladys said and put the kettle on the stove. As always, the kitchen was delightfully warm and Dory closed her eyes for a moment. She wasn't used to being out and about all day. "Lady Pettifer had Mrs. Parsons prepare a room for you upstairs."

Dory smiled tightly. The division between downstairs and upstairs, and where Dory belonged, had been a bone of contention in her relationship with the staff here. Technically she was here as Lady Pettifer's guest, even if she used to be a maid working here. The staff really didn't like ambiguity in station and tended to blame her for it. "That's lovely," Dory said.

"How are things in London?" Gladys said, her eyes large. "We hear such things."

"It is difficult, I won't lie," Dory said. "Downright hardship for many, but we pull through."

"I wish you could leave."

"It's where I'm needed."

"This horrid war simply stretches on and on. They tell us precious little of how things are going. Are we winning or not?"

Dory couldn't say. She knew little more than was reported on the wireless and that was so heavily censored it told them very little. "I understand the estate has been turned over to chicken-rearing."

"They'll sow the fields come spring, but we have thousands of them. A few have ended up in my pot on occasion, I must admit. They stay in the stables, those girls. Lovely most of them. I'm not supposed to cook for them, but I end up doing it quite often. They're given hardly anything to eat through their ration books. Not that it's easy to come by provisions, but the Lordship does have a tendency to get his hands on anything he wants.

A wedge of lemon drizzle cake was placed down in front of her and it was a sight to behold. With the small fork, she placed a bit in her mouth and flavor drowned her senses. Tartness and sweetness, and moist cake. "Oh, that's heavenly," Dory said wistfully. It reminded her of summer and innocent times.

Custard powder was part of their rations, which gave them a decent fruit crumble every once in a while, but none of them were particularly gifted in the kitchen. Their rations only provided one egg per week, so baking was a rare event. They spent quite a bit on their wages buying extra eggs on the black market.

"We have to be quite sparing with the sugar as the price is obscene."

"We haven't had an allocation in months," Dory stated. "Luckily, I haven't the worst sweet tooth, but Vera, a girl I live with, misses licorice something shocking. Not even the black marketeers can find her any these days."

Gladys smiled, but it faltered. "I do so worry for you. I worry for everyone these days. It's all I seem to do. Even the boys upstairs. Cedric is alright, but we rarely hear from Vivian. He's over in France somewhere."

"So I've heard. There hasn't been any news from him?"

"Not for a few months. I understand some aren't allowed to write for fear of giving something away."

Dory hoped that was the case and Vivian wasn't simply being thoughtless or self-absorbed. It wasn't something she could put past him, though. He had the propensity to be completely self-concerned.

Chapter 11

"HELLO, MY DEAR," Lady Pettifer said with a broad smile as Dory found her in the morning room. A tea service was steaming on the table between the white cane chairs. "I'm so glad you made it. I think the weather is about to take a turn. We do get some harsh winds here in winter."

"Lady Pettifer," Dory said and leaned down and kissed the woman where she sat. Her knees were probably bothering her in this weather, which was why she normally spent the winters at her house in the south of France.

Her loyal dog, Beauty, lay at her feet, getting up to greet the guest with a wagging tail. Dory put her fingers down for a quick lick as she sat down. "Hello, little one. I bet you miss Bellevieu as well."

"All these chickens are driving him to distraction," Lady Pettifer said, looking out the window at the endless coups outside. "But we must all do our bit, even if it stinks to high heaven."

Now that she mentioned it, there was a bit of a whiff in their air.

"When the wind changes," the lady said, "it can be quite unbearable."

"How is Livinia?" Dory asked.

"Well, besides the war, I think she is having the time of her life. They have been quite spared from the bombing where she is, except a few nights when those awful Germans are purposefully trying to hit Parliament or Buckingham Palace. The nasty buggers."

Dory smiled. That was the extent of Lady Pettifer's colorful language, but it still sounded so wrong coming from her lips. "Now tell me of this matter you are looking into."

"Well," Dory started. "As I mentioned, there was something very wrong about this body, this elderly gentleman."

"At sixty, he is hardly elderly," Lady Pettifer said and Dory felt admonished. Perhaps what really bothered her was referring to him as a gentleman. It was not a term used too liberally in her circles as it was elsewhere.

"This man, somewhere in his sixties, appeared to have been dumped on the site after the bombing, and all the experts I've spoken to seem to agree that there are odd circumstances around how he was found. But there was no identification and no one seemed to know him. However, the medical examiner said he had a recent appendectomy scar, which was apparently uncommon with a... a man his age.

"So I searched through the archives at the nearby hospital and eventually compiled a list of names of men around that age who'd had an appendectomy."

"Clever girl."

"It took some time, let me tell you, and I have no assurance he's even from the area."

"If I were to hide a body, I would hardly carry it across the whole city, though," Lady Pettifer said. "It would be too much of a risk with all the checkpoints and suspicious eyes. I would wager he's not from far away, carried there during the night, perhaps when everyone was hiding in the air shelters."

Dory stroked her fingers across her lips. It would be hard to drive an automobile at night in the sheer darkness. Because the streets were largely deserted except for the wardens, a motorcar had a chance of being noticed. Perhaps someone, a warden, had noticed a car that night on Pennyfield Street.

The other alternative would be that the man was carried on foot. Either way, if Lady Pettifer's assumption was correct, then he was probably delivered from somewhere nearby, and he was on the list of men she had in her pocket. In truth, she wasn't sure why she had brought it with her. It was of no use to her there, but then it was such a hard-won thing that she didn't want to risk it to the bombs that dropped every night.

"Is it truly awful down in London?" Lady Pettifer asked. "Livinia doesn't tell us anything."

"I am sure being in the War Office, her correspondence is heavily supervised. But yes, it is awful. Beautiful too, like the darkest and grisliest symphony you could imagine." Dory smiled tightly, a smile of sadness. "If only it would end. I don't know how long we can keep going like this."

"I hope this is not a risk to your sanity, my dear. I can write to Mr. Churchill and have him excuse you."

Dory chuckled. "I will manage like everyone else." They were silent for a moment. "I do appreciate the money you send every once in a while. Mostly it goes on buying eggs."

"You couldn't throw a stick without hitting an egg here."

"We lost our kitchen wall, did I tell you? Every afternoon, we sit and eat breakfast in sight of the whole street."

"I couldn't imagine," Lady Pettifer said with a shudder. "Now you mentioned you got a letter from that lovely detective."

"He's a captain now. Apparently, he will be in London for a short while some time towards the end of next week."

"I hope you will see him then. Perhaps he will take you dancing."

A blush crept up Dory's cheeks and she looked away, hating how she blushed so easily. "Somehow, I doubt he is a dancing man."

"War changes men," Lady Pettifer said. "Some become more serious, and some less so. He was a fairly serious man to begin with, so perhaps he has lightened a little."

"I hope so," Dory said—not because she thought he needed to be lighter; she just didn't wish him to be more serious than he was.

"Cedric is faring well," Lady Pettifer said about her oldest nephew. "They have given him more responsibility." It wasn't strictly mentioned anywhere, but Dory knew that the heirs to landholding titles were mostly excluded from the conscription. The aristocracy feared the turmoil to their class if all their heirs were killed in the war, but they were given responsibilities within the various ministries. Leisure wasn't allowed by anyone.

"Ah, I believe we have a visitor," a booming voice was heard from the hall and Dory turned to see Lord Wallisford, who seemed to have gotten rounder in the last two years. His wife's absence gave him freedom to indulge, it would appear. "And who might this be?"

"Miss Dory Sparks," Lady Pettifer said and Dory rose from her chair, putting her hand lightly in Lord Wallisford's.

"Enchanted. It is so rare we have visitors these days." It seemed the lordship had no recollection that she used to work as a maid here, or perhaps he chose not to show that he knew her, being that she had been instrumental in his wife's conviction of murder and social downfall. It had been a disgrace to the family. In a sense, it was miraculous she was allowed through the doors.

"Dory mans one of the searchlights down in London every night. Faces the Germans head-on."

This seemed to impress him. "Well, I help our guns find them."

"An essential job," he said.

Over time, Dory had started to wonder how effective they were, considering how few of the planes they brought down. It was the barrage balloons. In doing their job by stopping the planes from diving, they also kept most of them out of accurate range of the guns. It was a trade-off and Dory wasn't sure they were better off this way.

"What are we planning for supper tonight?" his lordship asked, turning to Lady Pettifer, who had apparently taken over the domestic arrangements. "Not more bloody chicken, I hope."

"I believe the village boys sold us a pike."

"Ah," Lord Wallisford said with a lightened mood. "I like pike. Something creamy with a bit of pepper. Gladys does know how to turn out a good fish course. Perhaps I should do some fishing myself when the weather permits."

"I am sure Gladys will be more than impressed. Mr. Holmes can likely chase down some rods and reels somewhere."

"Hmm," the man said and left.

"He's grown increasingly restless," Lady Pettifer said after he'd gone. "I worry about his nerves. He needs something to occupy him, so if he wishes to take up fishing again, I will wholeheartedly support it."

"And yourself. How are you?"

"I worry for Andrew, of course. And Vivian. Mostly Vivian, being over there doing God-knows-what. Aldus worries too. I think it preys on his mind. Alfred Morely from the village succumbed, we heard. Very sad. His mother is a good woman."

It was unlikely they had seen the messenger boys on the bicycles as they delivered bad news around town. Perhaps it was the stationmaster or the postman who delivered the telegrams up here. "I am sorry to hear that."

"You hear more and more of it," Lady Pettifer continued. "But it was like this during the Great War too. Every day." Twisting her napkin, she looked out the window. "I don't think we'll see the end of this for some time yet. I think we will see total and complete exhaustion before we see the end of this."

"I hope not," Dory said and meant every word of it.

Chapter 12

IT WAS STRANGE RESTING in a room she used to tidy. The lack of maids was showing in small ways all over the house. The whole house had a mustiness. Dory had to air her room out for a few minutes, even though it brought the cold and wind inside, and the wind had picked up dramatically. It pressed on the windows and whined along the hallway. Wallisford Hall was never a warm place at the best of times, but the fire soon warmed her room.

When it came close to supper, Dory went down to see Gladys, who wouldn't hear of accepting help. The looks from Mrs. Parsons stated that she was definitely not welcome downstairs, so she went upstairs again to wait for Lady Pettifer to come down.

The house was entirely quiet and mostly dark. In places, they didn't bother drawing the curtains, because they didn't bother lighting it. As she wandered, she could hear Mr. Holmes closing the curtains or shutters around the house. Even out here, blackout needed to be observed—as if the Germans would assume they were simply not there. In all honesty, the Germans were fairly good at finding their targets withstanding their efforts to appear camouflaged into the night.

There was an edge of ineffective paranoia to the directions they were given by the Ministry of Information. The worst was the flyers telling them how to behave, which were most annoying of all. In fact, they annoyed mostly everyone, especially when they utterly lacked common sense.

Walking along the hall, Dory slowly made her way to the parlor, passing a portrait of the lord's youngest son, Vivian Fellingworth, standing resolutely with a satisfied expression on his face. The artist had managed to capture him quite well, even the golden hue of his hair. It had been painted a few years ago. There was a youthfulness about him. He'd grown a bit since then, broadened in the face and shoulders.

Then Livinia, looking ethereal in a gauzy white dress. Carefree and elegant. Her portrait suited her well too.

"The wind is picking up something shocking, isn't it?" Lady Pettifer said as she walked down the darkened stairs. Dory hadn't heard her coming. "Damn Churchill for not allowing weather reports. How are we supposed to know how to manage our own business? It's not all about the Germans. There could be a full storm brewing and we are none the wiser."

"I hope not. I have to catch the train back in tomorrow."

"If it's a storm, I doubt the Germans are senseless enough to fly into it. I'm sure they won't need you."

"Doesn't actually matter. I have to be there all the same."

His lordship was heard on the stairs. "Now Gladys has prepared us some fish tonight, I believe," he said. He had to be speaking to Mr. Holmes, whose answer was inaudible. "There you are," he said when he appeared in the salon. "Drink anyone? Sherry, Constance?"

"Yes, we'll both have one."

"Cedric called earlier. I understand he is being sent over to Washington," he said as he tended to the bar, which was usually Mr. Holmes task, but Dory imagined he was needed elsewhere.

A small cut crystal glass with a flaring stand was given to her, half full of the garnet-colored liquid. It had been an age since she'd had a sherry. Not her favorite tipple, but one could not be fussy these days. "Thank you," she uttered.

"Apparently it has something to do with the work Henry Tizard was doing over there. Jet propulsion or something such."

"What on earth would they want Cedric for?" Lady Pettifer asked. "No one would accuse him of being technically minded."

"I don't know. They insist on keeping mum about everything, but I suspect they're really trying to overturn the Neutrality Act. Everyone wants that bloody act overturned. Roosevelt is proposing to sell munitions to us, but the isolationists are fighting him—as if there were such a thing as isolation in a war like this."

"Sounds like important work," Lady Pettifer said.

"Yes," Lord Wallisford said absently. "We simply don't have the resources to sustain this war if they don't come to the party. The majority of Americans support repealing it, but the problem with

American politics is that their factions are always so unwilling to compromise. It doesn't help that bloody Hoover has placed that Irish lout Joe Kennedy as their ambassador here in London. Refuses to help with anything. Made all his wealth selling alcohol during the prohibition, so he's never been much more than a criminal. Hates the English and he's never hidden that fact. Keeps telling anyone who'll listen that we will fold to the Germans by Christmas. They really should expel him from the country. In a time like this, it's criminal to exclusively care about one's own slights and prejudices. Ridiculous man."

Mr. Holmes appeared at the door. "Whenever you are ready," he said solemnly.

"About time, I'm half starving," his lordship said and they placed down their glasses and moved through to the dining room. The curtains had all been drawn tight and even in the large room, it felt a little claustrophobic. Candles sat along the large table and Lady Pettifer and her brother still insisted on sitting at opposite ends of the table, as far away from each other as possible. Dory had to sit in the middle, which still felt far from both of them.

"So, Miss Sparks," Lord Wallisford said. "How are things in London?"

"There is more and more devastation every night, but the worst is that the people who lose their residences have nowhere to go. There is no one available to rebuild."

"Miss Sparks lost part of her kitchen," Lady Pettifer added.

"Oh, I am sorry to hear that. The place must be riddled with crime."

"There is some, I suppose," Dory said. "Mostly people simply want to get on with things. There are not enough air shelters and the ones we do have are badly provisioned." She hadn't meant for it to be a session where she spelled out all the wrongs, but it simply flowed. "People are getting very angry about it—the lack of response and consideration from the Government."

"The Government can't solve all their problems for them," Lord Wallisford said.

"No, but they should ensure there are enough air shelters when the Germans are coming to bomb us every single night." The people of the East End were not people that he had a great deal of natural sympathy for, and sentiment of him and the people like him was picked up by the people in question, and anger was growing. "The people are experiencing a tremendous degree of strain. Being ignored in their suffering is not something they take kindly to."

"I'm sure no one is ignoring them."

"I would hope so, Lord Wallisford," Dory replied tartly, knowing that ignoring them is exactly what the Government had done. "Assistance is starting to filter through to the absolutely destitute, but not enough to rebuild their homes, and there are no homes to move into. Every day the housing stock is less and less. People end up living on top of the rubble of their former houses because they simply have nowhere to go, except a cramped air shelter where there aren't any latrines or even enough room to lay down. Night after night, it wears and I don't know how long they will manage."

So it turned out that this was the occasion when all her worries surfaced. These were the things she saw each day and she just didn't know how long the people of the East End could be left in this situation. "It was true that the war affects everyone and every single person have sacrifices they have to endure, but the people around where I live are suffering disproportionately. And that is simply fact."

The table was quiet for a moment. While her friendship with Lady Pettifer was always wonderful, the friendship with her class was typically a little more drawn. Vivian was always good at stoking that fire and poking fun at her and her bourgeoise attitude. 'Oik' was the term he'd used a time or two.

Perhaps she shouldn't speak like this, because neither Lord Wallisford or Lady Pettifer were responsible. They were both kind people. "I am sure the Government is working to rectify things," she finally said as a way of mollifying the discourse she had started. "As I said, things are wearing. I suppose my sensibilities included."

"Perfectly understandable," Lady Pettifer said.

"Will anyone be in need for second helpings?" Mr. Holmes asked. "If not, we will continue to dessert." He moved to clear the table away, which wasn't normally his job. Before the war, serving wine was his responsibility, plus shooting warning daggers at the maids for any misstep, but the whole supper service was completely up to him now.

Dory smiled, but she still felt uncomfortable being there, able to accept a second helping when so many weren't getting quite enough. Rations were never quite sufficient to sate hunger. Even so, her qualms about having more than others would not hold when it came time for another slice of lemon drizzle cake, and that was something she would have to live with. Everyone had their breaking point.

Chapter 13

THE WALK FROM THE Whitechapel underground station was long and in places, she had to turn back and find an alternate route, because there was too much rubble strewn across the street. Glass crunched under her feet wherever she walked. Even on the clear streets, there was debris everywhere, so it was faster to walk than taking the bus. In some areas, whole blocks had been razed to the ground.

Increasingly, the East End was looking more and more like a dump. Debris and sandbags. The normalcy of Wallisford Hall and Quainton quickly faded. For a little while, she had been able to pretend everything was normal.

Gladys had sent her home with a good portion of ham and cheese, which felt like gold in her bag. On her other hip was her ever-present gas mask. Wardens fined people if they didn't carry them. Not that anyone bothered to pay a fine these days.

The crater on her own street was there exactly as it had been the day it had happened. Although craters were good places to stash the debris, but no one had the time to address it. What was the point when there was another mess only yards away.

Vera and Betsy were in the small front garden where the tree trunk had finally been removed. "Hello," she said. "What are you doing?"

"Planting carrots," Vera said, standing up and stretching her back. Her hands were covered in dirt. "Apparently the Germans have sunk some supply ship and now we can't get tea at the shop. Half the things we have rations for, we still can't get, so we've finally conceded that we need to start making this small patch of dirt productive."

"I got some ham and cheese," Dory said.

"Brilliant. They have all sorts of things out in the country, don't they? Especially if you're going to visit fine country houses," Betsy said.

"Well, they're doing their bit too."

Betsy turned away for her snort, but Dory still heard it. *You can choose not to eat the ham and cheese if you like*, Dory felt like saying, but didn't. Instead, she walked into the kitchen and placed the ham and cheese into the warm ice chest. It had been a while since ice had been delivered, and granted, the food never lasted long enough to need cooling.

Sitting down at the table, she pulled out the note with the names of elderly men with appendectomies. There were twenty-three, which wasn't an insurmountable number. She just needed to start seeking them out. There were a couple on the way to the searchlight and she would try to find them on her way to work that evening.

Vera turned on the wireless and the tunes of a string quartet filled the room. "I wish they would play more gay music. It's always so solemn."

"Don't think the people at the BBC could handle anything more upbeat," Betsy said.

"Might be seen as unseemly."

Getting up, Dory went to the counter and walked over to the bread bin. The bread was hard and stale, but it was chewable, so she cut herself a thin slice of ham and placed it on top.

"Should we put the rest of the ham in a stew?" Vera asked. "We can have it for dinner. We have some potatoes and cabbage."

"Yes, let's," Dory said. There would simply have to be cheese sandwiches from now on.

"We're just about out of salt," Betsy said. "You didn't manage to get some of that, did you?"

"No, just ham and cheese."

"Shame."

"I'll go buy some salt." Lady Pettifer had also given her another five pounds, which she'd been reluctant to accept, but Lady Pettifer rarely took no for an answer. This wasn't something she was about to tell the girls, though. They struggled enough with her friendship with Lady Pettifer, and granted, so did most others too. "I might leave early for work. There are a few things I want to check."

"Still looking for that man?" Vera asked.

"Yes, well, I have a list of names and addresses now."

Moving to the hole in the wall, Vera looked up at the sky. "It's going to be a dark night. The Germans will give us hell tonight, I bet."

Taking a bite of her sandwich, Dory sat down at the table. And put little checkmarks next to two of the names on her list. Matthew Harrows and George Mason. After finishing her sandwich and having a bit of a wash up in her room, she would take off. She'd slept the entire train ride, so she felt quite refreshed. And salt, she had to get the salt.

*

A woman named Dellis opened Matthew Harrows' door. It was a typical brick two-story house with two windows upstairs and one large window next to the door.

"Good afternoon, I am looking for Matthew Harrows."

"Mr. Harrows died about a year back."

Dory's eyebrows rose. As he had been amongst the living records in the hospital archive, they obviously had wrong information. "Oh, I'm sorry to hear that."

"What you want with him?"

This question stumped Dory and she should have been more prepared. "Just making a welfare check," she said with a smile. "My records are obviously wrong. I'm new to this."

"Oh, aye," the woman said. "Well, he's gone." She closed the door and Dory stepped back from the stoop, crossing the name off her list. If he died a year back, he was definitely not the body in Pennyfield Street. It would even have been before the raids started. For a moment, she wondered if she should inform that man in the archives that the information was wrong. Maybe at the end of her investigation.

The first name was crossed off her list, so she continued to the next address, which was an old wooden building close to Poplar High Street. Dory immediately saw a fire hazard, but all buildings burned when hit by a bomb. The door was ancient and layers of smudge marks sat like a stain on the door frame. A pervasive smell of boiled cabbage seeped out as an old man opened the door. Turned out the smudge marks were on all over him too. Coal dealer, she guessed. "George Mason by any chance?"

"Who's asking?"

"Miss Dory Sparks, just checking records for the ATS. Have you got all the equipment needed to put out an incendiary bomb?" She should have brought some pamphlets to prove her cover, as she couldn't very well say she was investigating a suspicious dumping of a body.

"The whole back is stacked with coal. I doubt a bucket and a piddly water pump will do much if that lot sets off."

"Ah," Dory said, lost for words. Actually, that was a problem. The whole block would burn down if a bomb fell here. "I see." This was perhaps something the wardens would have to deal with. Hopefully they knew. "Someone might come speak to you about fire protection with your special circumstances. You are going to the shelter every night?"

"Why bother? I'm an old man. If the Germans bomb me, then they bomb me. Besides, it's better that I'm here in case an incendiary does drop."

"Of course," Dory said and then smiled. "Thank you for your time."

Another name crossed off her list, but she might have a talk with one of the wardens about the place when she had a chance. Stacks of combustible material was probably something that needed to be mentioned to someone.

Looking up at the sky, she saw that the sun was quickly setting. It was time to head over to her searchlight. She needed to clean the mirrors before the sunset. Orientating herself, she headed back to Poplar High Street, from where she could get on her path to work.

Dusk was settling as she made it there, and quickly opened the searchlight to access the mirrored panels that concentrated the light. Birds had made a mess on it during the day, so she was dealing with that when Vera turned up.

"It's going to be a messy night," Vera said, placing her thermos down. "I borrowed a couple of tea bags from Julia down the street. Do you want some?"

"I'd murder for a cup of tea," Dory said with a sigh, putting the carbon arc back in place. "We're ready to light up."

"Betsy is checking the electrics downstairs." Vera sat down on the canvas chair with her mug, handing the thermos over to Dory.

As darkness fell, they waited, but there was no word from Betsy and no siren came. Vera even went down to check that Betsy hadn't fallen asleep. "Nothing," she said. "Not a peep."

Looking up at the sky, there wasn't a star in sight and the moon was only a faint glow behind the thick cloud cover. "Why aren't they coming?"

"Maybe something has changed," Vera said. "Or perhaps they are running late."

"They're normally here at the earliest opportunity."

"Hopefully they all dropped dead."

Dory turned to look at her, her mind racing as she tried to understand. They had been bombarded every night without fail, except the really clear ones, but tonight it was eerily quiet. Most of London was still in their houses, waiting to be called to the shelters. Everyone was waiting for the awfulness to begin.

Chapter 14

THEY SAT ON THE roof all night and nothing happened. The light of dawn started creeping over the quiet city, followed by the sound of lorries and buses starting to rumble past.

Betsy finally emerged from downstairs.

"Anything?" Vera asked.

"No mention over the radio," she said and stretched.

In a way, it felt as though they had energy because the night hadn't been taxing. Normally, exhaustion dampened both their minds and bodies, but they'd just spent almost twelve hours being idle.

"I might go do some stuff on the way home. I'll get a cheese butty on the way," Dory said as she stood from her canvas seat. She might as well check some of the names on her list before going to bed.

Vera was packing her stuff and Dory turned off the auxiliary power to the searchlight. It felt strange walking away after a night of nothingness, but there was exhilaration on the street. It seemed most had enjoyed a good sleep in their own beds that night, or else a peaceful night in the shelter. People were out and about at dawn, celebrating a night of peace.

Dory couldn't help but to feel the elation as well. Could it be that these air raids would end? But her hopes were soon dashed by the paperboy emerging on the sidewalk. "Coventry smashed to pieces!" he yelled, holding the paper up in his hand, handing out copies to those who approached.

In a way, Dory wished she could bury her head in the sand and ignore this piece of news. They had been so elated that there had been a peaceful night, but it hadn't been. The Germans had just gone elsewhere. Reaching into her pocket, Dory pulled out a penny for a copy.

One thousand killed or injured, it said and Dory gasped. They wouldn't have expected it, and the death toll was devastating because of it.

"Good that someone else gets it for a change," a woman said with terse tones.

No, Dory wanted to argue. It wasn't good that anyone got it, but she did understand how the people around here were sick and tired of being the ones almost exclusively targeted by the Luftwaffe. *Night Raids Starting in the Provinces,* the paper went on to say.

Did this mean that they were going to hit every town in the country? It was horrible to think it, but from a strategic point, it was better if the Germans focused on one area, but perhaps they had decided they had destroyed everything they needed to here. Maybe they wouldn't be back.

For the first time, she worried about her mother. Surely they wouldn't bomb Swanley, but it was an irrational fear. Swanley was tiny. There would be no reason for the Germans to bomb there. It was nothing more than a little farming town. Still, though, everyone in the country would fear what tonight would bring if the Germans were seeking targets outside of London.

Tucking the paper into her bag, the elation she had felt at having a quiet night had now melted away and tiredness was nipping at her. Still, she wanted to cross at least one person off her list. Maybe she could check the two in Limehouse and then take the bus back. She could see the bus going there coming down the road, and that made up her mind for her. Picking up speed, she made her way to the bus stop just as the last person in the queue was stepping up on the back. Dory joined the end of the queue and tried to find a place for herself on the full bus as it traveled down East India Dock Road toward Limehouse.

Limehouse was as devastated as Poplar was, but she eventually found one of the addresses down along the River Lea. It was a nice area and she reached a large, whitewashed house—a respectable house. *Well, there was certainly some money here*, Dory thought as she looked up at the house. Money was always a motive for murder. Obviously, she was jumping to conclusions.

Knocking on the door brought a maid, who confirmed that Mr. Jones did indeed live there and he was very much alive. Another name off her list.

The second name was more complicated because the house was bombed. It hardly made sense that a body would have been pulled out of one ruined house to be placed in another. The neighbor also confirmed that the man had survived the attack and had gone to live with his sister in Bournemouth. Another name crossed out.

With her task completed, Dory returned to the main road and waited for the bus back. After sleeping, she might tackle a couple more that afternoon, but she was increasingly growing more tired now, even as the people around her were all rushing off to work. Everyone present and accounted for. No one had died that night. It was a wonderful feeling to think that.

At her stop, Dory got off and trudged up the street, knowing that her house would definitely be there, along with all the others on her street. Maybe with this reprieve, they could start to fix things, repair the crater in front of the house. That was probably wishful thinking, but someday, someday, the crater would be fixed and cars would drive along the street again.

With a sigh, Dory pushed open the ill-fitting door and stepped inside the quiet house. She could just walk straight into the kitchen, but it felt wrong. Pointlessly, she locked the door. Vera and Betsy were already asleep upstairs. The house was safe enough during the day. The neighborhood kept an eye on them while they slept, and at night, they locked the kitchen door to keep any opportunists out. So far, their stale bread had proven safe.

Trudging upstairs, she washed and fell into bed, for a moment staring at the list. Four names down. If she worked on it for the rest of the week, she would get through all of them.

*

Over the next week, she found a baker, a drunk, and a retired school headmaster who was no longer retired. Another administratively misplaced man who had died some time ago. A grocer, three dock workers, a member of the home guard and a bassoonist with the Royal Orchestra. One man was in his eighties and had taken a good five minutes to reach the door, all along yelling that he was coming. Dory felt bad having to drag him away from his comfort, but he insisted. It would take that poor man half the night to get to an air raid shelter. Most likely, he didn't even try.

There was no answer on many of the doors she knocked on, but she confirmed with neighbors that the person wasn't missing.

Before long, she was down to one name on her list—all the way over in Bethnal Green. It would take some time to get there, so she had left that one for last, and maybe that had been the one she was after all along. A nervous feeling had settled in her stomach. What if it wasn't him? Then she wasn't at all closer to identifying this man. He could be from out of town, or living in an entirely different part of the city. She would either have to give up or search through the records of other hospitals.

It was still hard to imagine someone taking a body across the whole city to dispose of. It could still have happened, though. In saying that, the man had looked local. He certainly hadn't looked like a resident of the West End. If the man was from nearby, the two hospitals he could have had been a patient at would be Guy's Hospital on the other side of the Thames, or Barts—but it would still be a very long way to cart a body during an air raid, with bombs dropping all around.

The bus to Bethnal Green took a long time, but she eventually got there and confirmed that Whitby Thomas, a man with a surname as a Christian name and vice versa, was indeed alive. The man found in Pennyfield Street was not on her list. It was disheartening; she'd been so sure she would find him, had thought herself too clever in the means by which she was going about identifying him, but it was all for nothing.

The poor man would probably never be identified. No doubt, he was already buried, and Dory was sure that someone was getting away with murder. It was a unique frustration. This poor man's life had been taken and no one knew. Well, she knew, but she had been unable to prove it.

Obviously, she could repeat the exercise with the other two hospitals conceivably within the region, but with the distance, her hope of finding him was diminishing. She would have to, not sure if she could live with herself if she didn't. Still, though, it felt more hopeless now than it did a week ago.

Chapter 15

WITH NERVOUSNESS Dory stood at Victoria station. Looking at the large crowded space, it wasn't perhaps a great idea to meet here. Everywhere she looked, she saw soldiers and she was looking for one in particular.

To be here, she'd had to trade a day off with one of the other ATS girls, which meant she wouldn't have another for a while. Going down to visit her mother in Swanley wasn't going to happen anytime soon. A little guilt Dory simply had to live with.

Some of the men were injured, limbs and heads bandaged. Dory hated seeing it. As with the people here in London, their men were being devastated overseas as well. The worst was that they knew very little of what was going on. Things were mentioned on the news—Egypt and Africa, Norway, but there was very little specifics and they said nothing about how the war was actually going.

By the looks of it, though, some of these men were tanned well beyond what the English winter sunshine would be responsible for. They must have come from down the Mediterranean or further south. Not all were injured. Most looked perfectly fine.

Dory studied them. They looked both tired and excited, many here for a few days of fun and entertainment. They were the ones filling the dance halls every night, getting as much enjoyment in before they had to go back. Captain Ridley too, here for a few days to get away from the war. If it weren't for the constant nightly bombardment, it would be easier to forget the war was on.

Finally she saw him and she stretched up on her toes and waved. He smiled when he saw her. As with some of the others, he was golden with sun.

"Miss Sparks," he said when he arrived and placed down a small suitcase. The greeting was a little awkward as they didn't really know each other well enough to embrace.

"Captain Ridley. It's good to see you. You look well." In a way, she both recognized him and didn't now that he stood right in front of her. It had been a long time since they'd seen each other. "I got your letter."

"And I did get yours, but not in time to write back. Shall we move away from here? Have you time?"

"Yes, I have all day. I don't need to be back at work until tomorrow night." That didn't sound forward did it? She hadn't intended on implying anything by it. As long as she'd known him, he'd never been the lewd type, which was probably part of the reason she was here.

If he read anything inappropriate into the statement, she couldn't tell, because he gently took her by the elbow and moved her away from where another wave of passengers was coming. "I need to drop my bag off at home, but after that, perhaps we could have a coffee somewhere."

"That would be lovely."

Outside the station, the traffic was mayhem. There were people going in every direction, soldiers being dropped off by family and friends, and soldiers being met in tender and sweet greetings.

"Is your family nearby?" she asked.

"My parents have passed," he said as he walked to a waiting taxi. "Pimlico," he said, urging her in. "My mother a few years back."

"I'm sorry to hear that."

The streets looked mostly clear of debris and Dory felt conflicted about it. In a way, it didn't reveal what was happening to London, but also, it would make it easier to forget the war for a while— something Dory wasn't entirely sure she could manage. "This part of London has fared better than the East."

"That is what I have heard."

"I trust you are well where you have been."

"Naturally, I cannot discuss it."

"Of course," Dory said. What she wanted to ask was if it was safe, whatever role he performed in this war, but she knew he couldn't even answer that. And who had any assurance in this war? Certainly not her. There was every chance a bomb would find her roof one night. Perhaps it was even inevitable. She refused to think about it.

They pulled up in front of a tall brick building. "Is this where you live?"

"I will drop off my bag. You can come up if you like."

If it was anyone else than him, she wouldn't, but she was so very curious. His flat was up five flights of stairs. "Quite a climb after an exhausting day," he said. The walls were painted white and their steps echoed as they climbed. "Although I am glad to see that the building is still here. I don't know what I would have done if it wasn't."

"I told you our kitchen wall is missing," she said.

"I recall."

"Our neighbors are very good at keeping an eye on the place when we are gone."

"That is kind."

"Well, you have to bind together in times like these."

They stopped at a wooden door and Ridley pulled out a set of keys and unlocked it. It had the stale air of a place that hadn't seen people for a while. The place was utterly still and silent. It was strange that this place sat here empty when there were so many homeless, but that was the way of things. Some had luck and others didn't. It wasn't her place to tell him that he should not have his apartment for his own use.

The sitting room had glass-paneled doors and parquet flooring. It was nice and bright, a lovely apartment. Her house was dark and cramped in comparison. "This is a lovely place." In fact, it was stylish beyond what she would expect from him. It was very arts décoratif, with elegant lines and simple décor.

"It originally belonged to my uncle and he left it to me after he died." Ridley disappeared into the side room and quickly returned without his suitcase. "Shall we go. There is a nice café down close to the river."

Dory smiled and followed as he led to the door. "How long are you staying for?"

"Four days, although two of them are not at my leisure."

"Oh," Dory said as they walked down the stairs. "I went to see Lady Pettifer the other week. She is doing well. The Ministry of Food has turned the whole of their lawn into a chicken farm. Not the fields, of course, just the lawn. Lord Wallisford has been forbidden to shoot anything, I hear."

Ridley smiled, but he didn't seem all that concerned about Lord Wallisford's chickens. Why would he be? Perhaps it was only Dory who found him being overrun by chickens amusing.

Besides the vast amounts of sandbags, the street looked very ordinary. They passed a woman with bright red lipstick, and Dory wished she had some herself, but hers had run out months ago. Cosmetics were typically snapped up as soon as any arrived, and they cost an absolute fortune.

"We've started growing our own vegetables," she said after a while. "The plot isn't large, but you can't always rely on the stores to have what you need. Do you have a rations book?"

"Somewhere," Ridley said. "Not planning to use it. I think I will eat out while I'm here."

"Of course," Dory said, feeling silly now.

The café was small and a few couples sat along the tables. "This is an Italian place," Ridley said, "but the owner has been interned. Shame. The man wouldn't harm a fly. His daughters manage the place now."

"Mr. Ridley," said a woman with lush, black hair, her smile beaming. She obviously knew him well. "It has been so long, and how handsome you look in your uniform."

The tight smile on Dory's lips belied the imposition she felt by this woman, and her overt familiarity. Clearly they knew each other. Did she flirt with him? Did he flirt with her?

"This is my friend Miss Sparks."

The young woman's beaming smile didn't falter and she greeted Dory like a long-lost friend. "I will make you some coffee," she said. "Sit, sit. We have pastries just coming out of the oven."

"No news of when your father is being released?"

"Nothing yet," she said with an exaggerated frown, "but he appreciated your letter of recommendation."

Ridley walked toward a seat that Dory suspected was his usual. "You come here quite a bit," Dory said. Obviously familiar with the family if he provided letters of recommendation for them.

"I do fairly often when I'm at home."

With a smile, Dory sat down and tamped down on the jealousy. It was probably perfectly normal, and it was only the easy charm and prettiness of the young lady that got to her. This was part of his life, she realized, and he was showing it to her. No need to ruin the gesture by sulking over how pretty the girl behind the counter was—or how familiar they seemed.

Chapter 16

"SO TELL ME ABOUT this body you found," Ridley said, stirring a spoonful of condensed milk into his coffee.

"Not found as such. I was simply walking past, but I noticed that he wasn't covered in dust like the others they pulled out of the same house. I didn't think it odd at the time, but later it struck me, and the doctor at the morgue agreed that it was unusual that a body should emerge clean, and unbeaten—he mentioned that too—from a collapsed house."

Ridley was listening, but giving her that blank expression he did whenever he questioned someone, as if he didn't want his own opinion to influence the person. "So you believe he was placed there."

"Yes," Dory said emphatically. "And no one on the street could place him at the house. The family kept to themselves and rarely had visitors."

"Doesn't mean they didn't on that night."

Dory continued without responding to that, because it just seemed strange that a family that never had visitors would on the one day the house was bombed. "The man had no identification on him. Nothing. The only distinguishing features was a scar from an appendectomy, which is apparently unusual in a man of that age."

"What age?"

"Sixties."

Ridley nodded absently as if he was thinking.

"So I searched all the records at the Royal London hospital, which serves most of the East End, for older men with appendectomies, which was quite a feat. But it did little good. All the men that had had an appendectomy at the hospital are in some way accounted for. It could be that he is from another area of London, but it's hard to imagine that someone would cart a body across all of London during an air raid. Of course, they would have to place it on the collapsed building between the time the bomb fell and when the rescue brigade arrived, but on a night like that, it would be hard to tell exactly how much time that would be."

"Anyone traveling during an air raid would draw attention," Ridley said. "It would be the time when unsavory characters would be out and about. Not everyone knows that, so it could well be that someone would think that would be a good time to drive across London. But it would be unusual that they weren't stopped and their details recorded."

Dory looked at him while she tried to think. She would never get access to those records. They would be intelligence. Ridley could, though.

"I don't have time," he said before she could asked the question. "Tell me how these men were accounted for."

"Well, I went to their address and knocked on the door."

"And they answered."

"Not always them. Sometimes others—a spouse, or a maid, neighbor."

"So you only have one account for each person?"

"Yes," Dory said.

"You have to get two. Anyone of those people could have lied and you have no way of corroborating it."

With a gasp, Dory's eyes widened. Ridley was right. It hadn't even occurred to her that someone could lie to her. They could have said anything and she just took it for granted, assuming they had no reason to lie. But it could well be that she'd spoken just to the person who had a reason to lie. "So I can't take any of those accounts for granted."

"No."

"I have to go find a second source."

"You're not suspicious enough," Ridley said with a smile. "You really should hand this over to the police."

"On what grounds would they even bother? A man was found in a building. There is nothing else I can prove other than a gut feeling that something isn't right. Yes, he was remarkably clean, but the police are so stretched these days, I don't think they have the time or inclination to look at this."

"But it's their duty to investigate crime, Dory, not yours." His hand slipped over hers and she felt the warmth of it. "This is not your responsibility. You need to take the case to the person responsible for investigating it. Hand over the list of men you gathered. I'm sure that will be very useful."

"I will once I have some kind of proof that there was a crime committed. There is nothing concrete."

"That is for them to determine."

"Would you investigate it if you were still a policeman?" she asked.

"I would find a second source to determine if the men on your list are indeed accounted for. If not, the man could be from anywhere. There are seven million people in this city. Sometimes, cases can't be solved, and you can't be an effective policeman if you don't accept that."

"I'm not a policeman."

"No, you are not. The police should make the call on how to proceed."

With a smile, Dory nodded.

"But you have excellent instincts," he said, leaning back against the bench and crossing his arms. Dory smiled brighter at the compliment.

Taking her cup, she took a sip of her coffee, which was much richer than any she'd had in a long time. They liked strong coffee down along the Mediterranean coast.

"Do you think this war will end soon?" she asked and Ridley's brow drew together.

"No," he said. "Not for a while yet."

"Lady Pettifer says four years. The Great War lasted four years."

"I hope not."

"Maybe if the American's come in, the German's will retreat. Lord Wallisford says that Roosevelt is favorable to the American's standing by us."

"So I have heard."

"I hope so too," Dory said. "I'm not sure how much longer we can take this bombardment. Food is getting scarcer—even with rations. And there are so many homeless people now. Tents are starting to appear in every park."

In a way, she hoped Ridley would have answers to these things, something that would give her hope, but he didn't.

"A lot hinges on the Russians, I think. Shall we walk for a little?"

Dory nodded and they rose to leave. "Has the Government really interred all Italian men?"

"Germans and Austrians too. Although mostly they are Jews, so the bulk of them will be or have been released, but not the man here."

"It was kind of you to send a letter to vouch for him."

"He is a good man. Good people get hurt by this war."

"Yes," Dory agreed.

For a moment, Captain Riley looked awkward, as if he didn't know what to do with leisure time. He was a hard man to imagine at leisure. "Do you want to walk along the river?"

"That sounds nice."

They walked in silence for a while. "Is it awful over on the continent? They tell us so little."

"There are a lot of desperate people."

As they had left Nice and Marseilles previously in the year, Dory had seen that desperation at the port—people trying to find somewhere to go and the Vichy Government refusing to let them, which had since been given the mandate by the Germans to govern over all of France.

Beyond that, Dory had heard little of what had happened to the area she had gotten to know so well, or the people that had been left behind. Who knew what awful things had befallen them. Maybe Lady Pettifer's chateau was nothing but a burned-out shell now, or even occupied by German or Italian military.

The world seemed so irretrievably different; it was hard to even imagine a world of peace again. It was a distant, shiny future that Dory would like to fully imagine. This war changed things; it was bound to. It couldn't just go back to the way it was, could it?

"Have you ever lived anywhere else but in London?"

"I was a constable in Oxford for a while."

"I have never seen you in uniform—other than right now, but that is different."

They walked past other couples doing exactly the same as they were, out for a day of leisure. Some looked a lot closer than they did. Exactly how close they were, she didn't know. What did this mean? Was there some closeness between her and Ridley? Was this day an indication that he saw her as something more than a friend? It was hard to tell. He wrote to her and had asked to meet her, but he hadn't specifically said anything about intentions beyond friendship.

Dory smiled at him.

"I understand most of the artwork in the museums have been carted away," he said.

"I believe so." At times, the conversation between them felt very stunted.

Parliament appeared along the river. The damage to Parliament had been reported in the papers, but Dory couldn't see it as it was on the other side of the building.

"Let's walk through Green Park," Ridley said and Dory smiled her agreement. It was a place she knew of, but had only ever run through. "We used to go quite often when I was a child."

"You grew up near here."

"Yes, my father worked in advertising," he said. "Fleet Street."

"My father passed away a long time ago."

"I'm sorry."

"Lung disease." It had been a while since Dory had thought about her father. He'd featured so little in her life, and she had barely any memories of him. Only a passing figure who came home after she had gone to sleep and left before she woke. Any spare time he had, he spent at the pub, rather than with his children. It was hard to miss someone she'd barely known.

Chapter 17

AS THEY WALKED INLAND beside Parliament, the large hole in the massive lattice window by the Old Guard square came into view. Most of the building was surrounded by sandbags. People and cars were coming in and out of the grounds, any debris from the bombing cleared away.

Crossing the square, they walked down along the Horse Guard, where a small group was practicing maneuvers on the large graveled parade area. It was nice to see something that was both extraordinary and perfectly normal. Men in fancy uniforms performing parade moves was simply not typical in her life. Ridley must have seen such things more often.

A blond woman in a smart fitted skirt and jacket walked toward them and then stopped. "Oh, didn't expect to see you here, Miss Sparks," Livinia said. "Extraordinary who you bump into some days. How are you? And the detective that came to our house. I see the acquaintance has extended."

Livinia looked very understated compared to her usual clothes, but she still managed to look like the daughter of a titled man. Bright red lipstick accentuated her lips and her hair lay in glossy curls around her shoulders.

"Miss Livinia," Dory said, a little taken by surprise. "Your aunt mentioned that you work around here."

"Aunt Constance can't keep her mouth shut," Livinia said tartly. "We're not supposed to mention what we all do, are we? I see you are in uniform, Mr... Sorry, what was your name again?"

"Ridley, Captain Ridley."

"Yes, of course. Lovely to meet you again." Besides the required politeness, Dory knew that Livinia absolutely didn't think so. Although very conflicted about Lady Wallisford's actions, Livinia in some ways blamed this man for bringing them to light. But the scandal of all that must be forgotten now that war had broken out. Too much water had flowed under the bridge, but there would be some who would never forget. "And I hear you are a brave girl and manning one of the searchlights every night."

"Yes, somewhat down the river."

"Even braver. Well, I must run." Lifting her hand off the black velvet clutch in front of her, she waved to a man on the other side of the street. Dory had never seen him before. Perhaps Livinia had a new beau, but then it was hard to tell as she had a multitude of male friends. This one, Dory hadn't seen before, but clearly of Livinia's set judging by the clothes, and a small, white dog on a thin lead.

"Well, it was lovely…" Dory said, but trailed off as Livinia jogged across the street and let the man kiss her on the cheek.

It was strange how they had been so close for a while, but now felt like complete strangers. Her friendship with Livinia had been a consequence of being thrown together rather than based on any true affinity.

Dory turned to Ridley and didn't quite know what to say. "That was Livinia Fellingworth."

"I remember," Ridley said. Holding his elbow out, he urged her to take it.

"Her brother Vivian has been neglectful in telling anyone where he is," she said, and wondered if Livinia knew. Working in the War Office, she might have access to such information, but then even Lord

Wallisford didn't know, and Livinia was frankly quite useless at keeping secrets. One had to wonder if someone had made a grave overestimation placing her in the War Office, but it could be that she had changed. The subdued clothes did go some way to say she had.

They kept walking to the park and stopped at a small bridge that looked back on Buckingham Palace. Apparently one of the guard houses had been struck there too, but it couldn't be seen from where they stood.

The trees were all without leaves and the pond water looked cold and still. Clouds had rolled in, making it dark. It was still lovely, though, as was wandering with no particular destination in mind. They walked over to a bench and sat down. Ridley went over to a cart and bought two steaming cups of tea.

"Will you return to your old role with the Met when the war is over?" she asked.

"That is the intention."

"I have no idea what I will do," Dory admitted. It was unlikely she would return to being Lady Pettifer's companion, but she hadn't particularly settled on a career to follow either. It had been interesting working in the munitions factory, turning up every morning and doing a full day's work. Perhaps she would work in a factory again once the ATS was done with her.

"I thought we could have dinner at one of the restaurants," Ridley said, distracting her from her musings.

"That would be lovely."

"Maybe walk a little further and then go."

"Not one for dancing and drinking, then?"

"Do you want to go dancing?" he asked, and she could see the discomfort in his eyes.

"Not particularly," she said with a smile, "but it's the only thing the girls I live with do on their days off."

"Not much of a dancer?"

"I suppose there are those who feel this is the occasion to dance, and I completely understand that, but I struggle to."

Normally Dory would be rushing to get ready for work now, and she felt guilty for not being there, but everyone had the odd day off, particularly if their… friend came to town for a few days off. Sadly, they could only spend this one day together as she had to work the next evening.

"Come, let's walk," he said, taking the now empty cup out of her hand, "and then we'll find somewhere warm."

It had grown markedly chilly as the sun was starting to set, being as it was late autumn, quickly hurtling toward winter.

They walked down the Mall, then found a restaurant just off Piccadilly. It was a lovely place with a Victorian glass roof that had somehow managed to survive months of bombardment. Palms stood around the space, elegantly bending their fronds down for admiration. The tables were small with wooden chairs. It was packed with men in green uniforms, attending their dates for the evening, a joyous atmosphere where people laughed and talked.

They ordered lamb cutlets with mash and gravy. And it was all wonderfully flavorful. She didn't dare think what this meal would cost, but it wasn't the night to worry about frugality. This was Ridley's only night out, and he was spending it with her.

"Are you spending the rest of your time back here in London?"

"No, but I cannot tell you where I'm going."

"Of course," Dory said. While she completely understood the need for secrecy, there was still that part of her that felt he should know that she would never betray a confidence. But she also respected him for not wavering on the rules.

They had glasses of wine and savored them as long as they lasted—until the air sirens sounded. Some rushed up to leave at once, deserting their meals. Others took their time, but the waiting staff were eager to close down.

"What do you want to do?" Ridley asked as they were gently ushered outside.

If she went to the shelter, it would be the only time she had, and it would be a shame spending the rest of her time with him crammed into a dusty and claustrophobic shelter. "I'm happy to do whatever you want to do. Obviously, I never go to the shelters."

"Then dare we brave it? I haven't experienced the air raids."

For a moment, she'd wondered if he'd force her down to a shelter as he seemed to be very particular about her safety. Tonight, though, he didn't want to spend the night in a shelter either.

People were running along the dark streets, seeking a burrow to spend the night in. Yawning children being pulled by their mothers and cars disappeared off the streets.

"Let's return to the river," Dory suggested, in a way feeling like she wanted Ridley to see what they experienced here every night. The Westminster Bridge would give them the best vantage point of what was the brutal and beautiful light display that was an air raid.

They walked in silence, an air warden ordered them to get somewhere safe from across a street, but neither of them wanted to. Maybe the war had changed Ridley's view of safety. Or perhaps it was hypocritical pushing her into a shelter when she stood on a roof making herself known to the Germans every single night.

The drone of the planes could be heard when she and Ridley reached the bridge standing strong over the inky blackness of the Thames below them.

"They are coming up the river tonight," Dory said. "They do that quite often." From where she stood, she could see the searchlights shifting across the sky. "I think that's my one," she said, indicating a distant light. It was hard to tell from here as there were quite a few. Vera was doing her job that night.

The Bofors guns started firing and the glowing hot steel lit up patterns in the sky. The noise of the air raid started, but there was often a lag between seeing a bomb drop and hearing it. The trailing flares of the bombs, the glow of the fires and the whistle of falling missiles.

In all this, Ridley put his arm around her shoulder and she let him. None of this was safe, but she felt safe with him there, as if she didn't mind what happened as long as they were together.

"You are a very brave girl," he said.

"You get used to it."

"I hate seeing this happening to my city."

Drawing herself closer to him, she felt him along her body. They had never been this close. She could smell his cologne. His eyes sought hers in the darkness, then he leaned down and kissed her. Dory's eyes swam closed and for a moment, she forgot everything else.

Chapter 18

"DORY," VERA CALLED from outside her door. "It's time to go. Get up sleepyhead."

Sitting up abruptly, Dory tried to gather her senses. She and Ridley had walked and waited until dawn for the bus that would take her back to Poplar. It had been bittersweet saying goodbye, because she didn't know when she would see him again. Or worse, she didn't know *if* she would see him again, but she had to get home and back to her duties.

With a staggering step, she got out of bed, feeling a little groggy, being pulled out of sleep in the middle of a dream. "I'm coming," she said and pulled on her trousers and blouse. Through the window, she could see that the sun was going long and dusk was approaching. There may not be time for breakfast.

Lacing up her boots as quickly as she could, she was ready, just about forgetting to brush her teeth in her rush. She wondered if Ridley had woken yet. It had been a lovely night, even with the terrible things going on around them, they had talked and laughed. It was a strange notion, insisting on getting on with life when so much was happening. Even with everything they had both given as part of this war, there was guilt for taking a moment for themselves. But that interlude was over now. It was time to get on with doing her bit for the war.

"I'm here," Dory said as she entered the kitchen. There was a lorry outside. "Are they finally fixing that hole?"

"I think they're starting," Betsy said as she handed Dory a wrapped sandwich. "Cheese. We don't have anything else."

"Thanks."

"We should go," Vera said as she grabbed her bag. "Hopefully it will be a quiet night tonight. We can always hope."

"So tell us about your night off with your beau," Betsy teased.

"He's not my beau," Dory said, but then wondered if he actually was. They had kissed last night, standing on the Westminster Bridge. "We walked mostly. Around Soho. I have to admit it was relatively quiet over that part of town."

"Because they're still bombing us to smithereens."

"Are you going to see him again?" Vera asked.

"No, he has to get back to his duties."

"Which is what exactly?" Betsy asked.

"Don't be so nosy," Vera reprimanded.

"Apparently I have been going about my investigation all wrong," Dory admitted. "Amateur mistakes."

"That's what happens when you're an amateur," Vera said. "I know we've given you a lot of flak about your sleuthing, but I do respect that you are trying to find out what happened to this man. There are so many people who are just getting lost in this constant bombing. There was this woman on Radish Street, I heard about. Pretty, young girl in a red coat and no one has a clue who she was. Her family don't know she's dead and they might never know what happened to her. Everyone should be forced to wear some ID at a time like this. At least this man has you watching out for him."

It gladdened Dory to hear that they at least understood what she was trying to do. For a while, she'd assumed that they were ridiculing her. Well, they had been ridiculing her, which was fine as long as they understood the importance of what she was doing. And even with what Ridley said, she was happy to hand it over to the police if there was enough to ensure they would actually look into it.

*

Throughout the night, Dory swung between nervous distress when the bombs were falling, to nervous delight whenever she thought of the kiss she'd shared. It was her first real kiss and at times it was hard not to think about it.

Eventually the Luftwaffe retreated and the all-clear sirens wailed. The city could now get on with dealing with this latest set of damage. The rescue brigades were out, as were the firemen, and the dawn of a new day broke.

As with every morning, Dory was exhausted, but she sat down and reviewed the list of names she had just about discarded when everyone had been accounted for one way or another. Now she had to remember all of them. She had only crossed names off, thinking she didn't need to record any more information. If she had been forethinking, she would have recorded more about them. Who she'd spoken to and what they said. Now she only had a list of names with nothing but lines.

When he worked as a police officer, Ridley had a notebook where he meticulously took notes. Maybe she should do the same thing, and not be completely reliant on her memory.

Some were easy to dismiss, such as the coal merchant. She'd spoken to him in person, so he could reliably be ignored from now on—unless it hadn't been him, and instead some other person pretending to be him. It sounded outlandish, but it would be the length a murderer would go to. Was it reasonable to insist on checking the identity that people gave her in person? Was that normal procedure? She didn't know.

In a way it was rude to go skulking around someone's neighborhood, asking people to confirm that so and so were who they claimed to be, but what choice was there? It was what policemen did. They couldn't afford to worry about rudeness, and neither could she. Still, it could make her uncomfortable. Even the coal merchant could be lying to her. For all she knew, he had a brother that had been so fed up for whatever reason, he saw it as a brilliant time to dispatch his sibling over the future ownership of their dirty coal empire. It sounded ludicrous, but apparently people murder for ludicrous reasons.

Vera and Betsy were gone by the time Dory was done with her review and she had the rooftop all to herself. Boats were starting to travel down the Thames, sailing into the ravaged docks. The Germans didn't stop them using the docks. It was a point of pride.

Making her way downstairs, she walked down to the high street to the stationary store, where she bought some more writing paper and a spiral bound notebook like she'd seen Ridley with. Then she went to the mobile canteen and bought a cup of coffee. The money Lady Pettifer sent her allowed her some luxuries that her ration-book wouldn't.

Pulling a pencil out of her bag, she started listing what she remembered about each man on her list—especially the ones she hadn't spoken to in person. It might even be that she needed to check the veracity of the ones that had been proclaimed dead. How easy was it to lie about that?

Dory's problem was that she tended to believe what people told her and it wasn't in her nature to question the truth of what she was told. Even with her investigations, it surprised her whenever a murderer was revealed. She never ended up seeing it coming.

Looking across the street, she let her eyes observe the things around her. The merchants putting out their wares, women running along to their jobs and a newspaper boy touting for customers. London was awakening. Not being a native Londoner, it had taken her some time to feel the city's charm, but she was starting to feel a little like she belonged here.

It may well be that she ended up staying in London. Her stomach lurched like she went over a dip in the road, because who knew what her future would be? Perhaps there was potential with one who'd so sweetly kissed her the previous night. That would mean staying in London. But the future was too abstract to think about.

The idea of meeting someone, or being with someone, had always been there in the back of her mind, but it also seemed so very strange. And to potentially be the wife of someone like Captain Ridley, well, that was… beyond anything she had ever hoped. He was such a lovely man, a respectable man who was strong and capable. And handsome. She could hardly forget handsome.

Still, she wouldn't tell Lady Pettifer about the kiss. In fact, she wasn't going to tell anyone about that kiss. A memory that was all hers.

Her eyes lingered on the general merchant's shop. A tray of freshly baked bread being carried in and Dory could smell it from across the street. Some bread would be lovely, but there was no point going in there as they only served the people assigned to the shop. Each person had their shop where their rations were registered.

For right now, she had an investigation to repeat, and she was going to do it right this time.

Drinking the last of her coffee, she handed back the mug to the woman in the van, and put her notebook away for her walk over to the coal merchant. Might as well start with him. And his local shop would have known him long enough to confirm if something strange was going on or if George Mason was in fact exactly who he said he was. She was fairly certain already, but this was about proper procedure.

Chapter 19

RETURNING TO THE STREET that Mr. George Mason lived in, Dory continued walking past his house where the door was firmly shut to the shop further down the street. There was a queue outside, which wasn't by any means unusual, but it was a long queue.

"What do they have?" Dory asked the harried woman standing in the back with a toddler on her hip.

"Sugar," she said.

"Oh, that's nice." Shame this wasn't her shop. It was rare that sugar came in, so it was understandable that so many people came. Perhaps if Dory and the girls were lucky, they could get some too.

With a smile, Dory walked along the queue to the front, suspicious and curious glances being thrown her way, even with her ATS uniform. No one said anything, but she could feel all their urge to object when she squeezed past the queue into the shop. The shopkeeper was an older man with a white apron. A small scooper in his hand poured glistening white sugar onto the scales, precisely measuring the amounts allowed each patron.

"Excuse me," Dory said.

"What you want?" the man asked brusquely.

"Is there a man by the name of George Mason around here?"

"Just down the road."

"Have you seen him recently?"

"Saw him this morning," the woman at the front of the line said. "What'd you want with him?"

"Just to order some coal," Dory lied.

"There's a sign just down the road. Don't know how you could have missed it."

"Registered here, then?" she asked, turning her attention to the shopkeeper.

"That he is. Got his yesterday."

"Right, thanks," Dory said and smiled. That was all the confirmation she needed.

"Dozy girl," she heard the woman say when she walked out of the shop, where people were eyeing her hands to make sure she didn't cut the queue for her rations.

Stopping somewhat down the road, Dory made notations in her notebook. George Mason could definitely be crossed off her list.

Her intention had been to do another one, but there was sugar available and that was not an opportunity missed for any degree of murder and mayhem.

*

"I think there's sugar at the shop," she said, bypassing the door and going straight to the hole in the wall. "I'll go." It was her turn anyway.

Quickly, she was handed their ration books and she marched down the road. It seemed she wasn't the only one who knew there was sugar. The queue was now longer than the store near George Mason's house. This was going to take a couple of hours at least. Dory was going to be exhausted and famished by the time she got home, but sugar had to be grabbed before it was gone. She passed the time considering what they could do with it. They had a pamphlet at home, explaining how they could make an eggless sponge.

Eventually, it was her turn and she placed the three ration books down on the counter. "We'll have our portion of sugar."

Mr. Henry nodded and went to scoop sugar into the scales. It looked so pure and beautiful. "There you are," he said, placing the paper wrapped bundle on the counter in front of her.

"What else do you have?"

"Powdered eggs." Even the mention of them made her throat restrict with revulsion. "Some parsnips and carrots."

Beside her was a new pamphlet from the Ministry of Food, suggesting a recipe for carrot marmalade.

"And this," Mr. Henry said, putting down a round can in front of her. "Ham."

"In a can?" Dory said incredulously. "It says Spam."

"Spiced ham. Twelve points." That was expensive. "Quite nice, some say."

"Alright, I'll take one."

"Spread it evenly over the books?"

"Yes, please. And a loaf of bread, two each of the parsnips and carrots." Dory said and packed away her horde.

"You know you can eat the tops of the carrots."

"So I understand," Dory said, feeling that little bit guilty because she never could bring herself to eat the carrot tops. "Thank you. Any news what is coming in next?"

"Potatoes coming tomorrow."

"Good," Dory said and stepped aside for the anxious person behind her.

They had sugar. It was a good day, and whatever Spam was. Dory wasn't entirely sure, but there was a plate of cut slices on the label.

The girls had already gone to bed, so Dory unloaded their provisions and went upstairs herself. The long day had taken everything out of her and she flopped into bed without bothering to undress.

*

It was past three when she woke up, which was a little later than usual. Vera and Betsy were talking down in the kitchen as she righted herself. She really should have taken the time to undress before bed.

Now she had to wash quickly before redressing. Her uniform needed a wash, but she was caught for time trying to do her investigation while also coming home to wash her clothes. In this weather, they would hardly dry in time.

"And what in the world is this that you got us?" Vera asked when Dory made her entrance into the kitchen. She placed down the can of Spam.

"Mr. Henry seemed to think they are worth it."

"Shall we open it? We only have one egg to share between us. We could scramble it and put it on a sandwich, I suppose."

Bringing out the can opener, Vera worked around the edge of the can, which released a meaty smell. It made a gloopy sound when it came out, keeping the shape of the can as it did. But it was pink.

"Made in America," Betsy said, picking the empty can up. "On the tin, they bake it whole."

"We don't have time to bake anything. Maybe we can fry it in the skillet like you do with ham steaks."

Dory sat down to review her notebook, while Betsy and Vera explored the new supplement to their groceries. "It's quite salty, isn't it?"

"It's nice enough."

"Only the Americans would put ham in a tin."

"It must have come right across the ocean."

Dory decided that she would go find Mr. Dellow that day before work. Hopefully she would have time to go to one of the restaurants as well, maybe have some pilchard and potatoes to keep her going through the night.

Before long, a sandwich cut in half was put down on a plate in front of her and she picked it up and bit into it. Saltiness was what she noticed first about the ham. It had a unique taste, but it wasn't bad. Not exactly ham as she knew it.

"Do you think it will become a staple down at the shop?" Betsy asked.

"I doubt it," Vera said. "Maybe every time we get sugar, we get cans of these."

"They take twelve points per can," Dory added.

"That's murderous," Betsy gasped.

Well, it was definitely edible and Dory felt full when she finished, which was nice. "I better go," she said, taking the plate over to the sink and wiping it clean.

"And where are you running off to now?" Vera asked.

"To find a Mr. Dellow to see if he is still alive." The old note she had with the names and addresses had become tattered now and she didn't need it as she had transferred all the information to her new notebook.

"Good luck," Betsy said. "Although I am glad I am not spending my spare time chasing ghosts."

"I'm not chasing a ghost," Dory said, defending herself. "I am chasing a murderer."

"Such melodrama. You should consider a career on the stage."

It was jesting, but it took some work not to be offended. She had thought they were supportive of her efforts, but they seemed to have slid back into ridiculing her for it. "Maybe I should," she said, although a career on stage was absolutely not for her—not that she could even contemplate a career after the war. She just didn't have that thing she was really passionate about. Other girls wanted to be hairdressers or secretaries, nurses—or to be on stage.

Dory had never had that, even as a child. Had always simply gone along with what was asked of her. Exactly as she had done when the ATS had come to the munitions factory, or when Lady Pettifer had asked her to be a companion. Coming here to man the searchlight had not been something she'd sought. The opportunity had simply presented itself, and she had agreed.

Grabbing her bag, Dory said her goodbyes and walked out the door. It was a nice day, clear—which meant it might be a quiet night. Hopefully, because Dory felt tired—a tiredness that she wasn't getting enough sleep to fix. She was taxing herself running around investigating this man's death every spare minute she had.

Still, the idea of this man being murdered and simply forgotten by everyone drove her on. It was a concept that always drove her on. It had in the past and it still did. The idea of being forgotten and ignored, your very life stolen from you. That wasn't something Dory felt she could ignore. And really, it was only a few more days to establish that the people on her list were definitely where they were supposed to be.

Chapter 20

DESPITE THE COLD, it was a clear, sunny day. It was a day where most people who could, wanted to spend the afternoon outside of their houses after a long, wet autumn. The weather lifted everyone's spirits—particularly as most hoped there would be no visit from the Luftwaffe that night. Hopefully the clear weather held, although it would be a freezing cold night if it did.

A woman was darning socks on the stoop of her house, taking in the warming sun on her pale legs. New clothes couldn't be found for love or money these days, so even the most tattered socks had to be repaired. Dory smiled as the woman looked up and turned her attention down the road.

The street she was looking for was around the corner, where a Mr. Dellow lived. Sadly, Dory couldn't remember much about her initial visit here, but she had crossed him off her list. It wasn't until she turned the corner and saw the place when she recalled that he hadn't answered the door and a neighbor had told her he wasn't home.

Instead of going back to the house in question, she went straight to the corner shop and again walked past the queue, which was significantly shorter than the one she had tackled that morning. They must have run out of sugar.

This shopkeep was thin with a receding hairline. Dory pushed her way through the queue to quiet grumbles.

"I am looking for Mr. Dellow," she said. "Is he by chance registered here?"

"He is," the man said.

"Have you seen him the last few days?"

"People come and go all the time. I can't recall such things."

Dory smiled tightly. This wasn't very helpful. "When do you think you saw him last?"

"Couldn't tell you," the man said and Dory realized he was just an unhelpful type. Probably wouldn't help with a glass of water if she was on fire. She'd met the type before, the kind who did nothing more than they had to, and she was more than grateful that he wasn't responsible for catering to her ration book, because he would probably do all he could to cheat people out of what they were due simply because he could. Everyone knew that most shopkeepers had a stash under their counter for people who were willing to part with more than the official price.

With a sigh, Dory turned back to the line of people. "Anyone know Mr. Dellow?"

"Lives down the road, the house to the left. Green sashes on his window."

Dory tried to focus in on the man who'd spoken. "Seen him lately?"

"Couldn't tell you, just got back into town from up north."

"He usually spends some time in the library down towards the high street, I think."

"Thank you," Dory said. None of this was the confirmation she needed.

Exiting the shop, she walked back toward Mr. Dellow's house and opened the small gate to the tiny front yard. There was no sign of anyone inside and no one came as she knocked on the door. Looking down at her feet, she waited, but no one came.

Next door, the curtain twitched slightly, but no one came out.

Taking a step back, Dory looked up at the upper windows, but there was no indication of anyone looking outside, and the bay window at the front of his house had net curtains which stopped her from looking inside.

There was nothing to indicate anything. Even the street was surprisingly quiet. There was one woman down the street, tending her small garden, but otherwise, most houses looked locked and deserted. Clearly people were working.

Dory walked toward the only woman outside. "Hello, there. I am looking for Mr. Dellow, who doesn't seem to be home. You don't by any chance know where I could find him, do you?"

"Sorry, I've just moved into the street. I lived some streets down until my house got bombed."

"Oh, I'm sorry to hear that."

"This is my sister's house. She might know, but she'll be at work for hours yet. Don't come home until past eleven sometimes. I don't suppose you could call back then?"

That would be quite impossible. "Hopefully that will be unnecessary," Dory said, but wondered if she might have to speak to this woman. Sunday would be her day off. Actually, depending on the woman's work, that might not be the case. "Thank you for your help," Dory said before walking away.

Looking around, there seemed no one else around. Who would have thought it would be so difficult to find someone to speak to. Maybe a warden, but they weren't out this time of day. They came out after hours, and she was working then.

In the end, she had to give up. Well, she wasn't giving up, but there was nothing else she could do right then. She wrote in her notebook that she needed to come back to this one, and told herself that perhaps she would address the easy ones before narrowing down to the ones that were difficult.

There was one more on her list for that afternoon, which was simply getting confirmation that the man was who he said he was, and the first person she asked was happy to do so. This one could be crossed off. Turned out some of them were easy.

On her way to work, she forewent the intended pilchard meal and picked up a cup of pea soup, which was warm and filling in the rapidly cooling evening. It wasn't until now that she noticed how cold her fingers were as they stung a little with the warmth of the cup.

"Any luck?" Vera asked when Dory walked onto the roof.

"Still not home, and there was no one there to ask. So Mr. Dellow is still unaccounted for. I'm sure the neighbors saw me, but they didn't come out."

"If it was the same one as before, they knew why you were there. Might not have had anything more to say."

"Could be," Dory agreed.

Dusk was painting beautiful colors across the sky. She'd never paid attention to dusk as much as she did here, regularly standing on the roof, waiting for evening to come.

"I think we'll have a quiet night," Vera said, sitting down in the canvas chair that creaked with her weight.

"I hope so."

"Betsy said it's very quiet."

The evening stretched on, and as expected, there was no attack that night. Didn't mean the Germans didn't go elsewhere where there was cloud cover. It made sense now that the Government refused to release the weather report. Why hand Germans the knowledge of where to strike? This way, they had to find out for themselves, which they seemed to manage well enough. They had to have spies all over the country.

Everyone was terrified of spies, suspecting everyone they met. 'Loose lips sink ships,' the saying went.

The stars came out and shone brightly in the sky as the city was plunged into darkness. The moon revealed the skyline of the city, but as with every night, each light in the city was quelled or covered. Even the cars that drove around at night often had hoods for the headlights so they shone only at the street directly in front of them.

Tucking her hands under her arms, Dory walked around, wishing they could light a fire. It was freezing that night. Plumes of steam came with every exhale. Gingerly hopping from one foot to the other, Dory tried to get her blood moving.

She wondered where everyone was that night. Ridley. In the morning, he would be going back to wherever it was he spent his time. Somewhere south, somewhere with sun that tanned him. Livinia, who was probably somewhere in the city, dining with her friends. Lady Pettifer who was likely in bed in Wallisford Hall. Vivian who stubbornly refused to be in touch, making them all worry—even her. Who would have thought she would at one point worry about Vivian Fellingworth?

Dory's brother might be working. At the tender age of sixteen, he had been sent to work in the mines, and from what she understood, they worked around the clock. It was a horrid job, but the country needed coal, more than they needed him as a soldier, and as selfish as it was, she was glad. It was the most horrible thing in the world to send their boys and men over to the continent to fight.

It was hard not to hate the Germans for doing this, for causing this. They had to be stopped. There was no other option. What everyone feared, though, was the day they crossed the Channel and invaded. Dory for one would pick up arms if that happened. How could she not? The insistence that women should not fight could surely not hold if the Germans invaded. Perhaps they were plotting it as she stood there in the moonlight, trying to keep warm.

Chapter 21

NOTHING MADE TIME drag as much as standing on a freezing cold roof all night. As they watched, the moon shifted across the sky and finally settled. It felt like merciful release when the light of day started cresting the sky.

"Well, let's hope it stays clear for a while," Vera said. "I think we need to bring more blankets tomorrow."

"Good idea. I am chilled to my bones."

As the stars faded, the sun lit up the skies in pinks, purples and mauves. Hopefully the sun would be strong enough to provide a bit of heat on such a winter's day—enough to melt the frost that had settled everywhere.

Walking down the stairs, Dory's knees felt stiff and creaky, wondering if she should get some more of that pea soup to warm her. It was a bit rich for breakfast, though. Maybe a warm ham butty and a cup of coffee. That sounded divine.

The mobile canteen was just setting up and they had no coffee that morning, only tea. Dory ordered one.

"I'm going to my mum's," Betsy said and ran across the road, leaving Vera and Dory sitting on a low wall, the cold of the bricks seeping into their backsides.

"I think I need to buy some mittens," Dory said.

"Good luck trying to find some."

"For once, I wish I had actually taken up knitting."

Maybe she should ask Lady Pettifer to lend her a set of gloves. Dory knew she was happy to help, but she hated asking. Normally it wasn't an issue, the great searchlight was hot enough for her not to need a coat most of the time, but on the clear nights when nothing happened, they just about froze.

"Are you going home or are you sleuthing again?" Vera asked.

"I am going over to the River Lea."

"That's quite a walk."

"There was a man there who I need to see. I only spoke to the maid."

"Murdered by the maid. What a way to go."

Dory chuckled, because she could actually see how a member of staff could murder their employer. There had been an odd time or two when she would quite happily have murdered Vivian. "Most murders happen by someone in the house. Mostly the wife or husband."

"Familiarity breeds contempt."

With a frown, Dory ate her butty. How awful would it be to exist in a marriage where one or both parties wished the other dead?

"Forty years of being married to someone and finally they snap. That last time of dragging mud onto the carpet, or slurping their tea, and the final straw is broken," Vera said. "My bet is on the wife."

"To drag the body all the way from River Lea to dump at Pennyfield Street."

"No need to ruin it with practicality. My bet is still on the wife. If she didn't do it, she wished she'd done it. Mark my words."

"Maybe marriage isn't for you, Vera."

"I've been wondering the same myself recently. Have you been wondering about what you're going to do after the war?"

"Unfortunately I still think that is a long time coming."

"I hope not. We could all be living under German rule, forced to marry some of those kraut-eating bullies."

"We'll all fight to the last bullet," Dory said.

Vera toasted her mug to hers. "Yes, we will. I better go. Mrs. Rosen wants me to help her move some furniture."

"Give your cup to me. I'll return them," Dory said and finished her own tea.

Before long, she was walking down the high street toward Limehouse. The neighborhood she was visiting was nicer than some of the others, and she wasn't sure that Mr. Jones would appear at the local shop at all. His staff would do his shopping for him, so she wasn't sure how she could corroborate the story that he was there.

Perhaps she simply should insist on seeing him, but it was too early to call on someone. Maybe if she waited, she would see him appear and go to work. Then she could approach him on the street and confirm his identity. Being a man of that age, he could be retired, but no one retired in this war.

Taking a seat on a bench further down the river, she watched the house and intermittently the barges that had started moving along the still, early morning waters of the river. Birds were noisily taking their places and Dory had to tell herself off for getting distracted.

Neighboring men started appearing out of their doors, wearing trench coats and hats, carrying umbrellas. This was a fairly well-off neighborhood of clerks and accountants. On the other side of the river were warehouses and offices. Import and export businesses as the city's goods came through this area. Where London traded with the rest of the world.

But Mr. Jones' door remained stubbornly closed. Finally it opened and a woman stepped out. By her clothes, Dory knew this wasn't the lady of the house. She was not dressed in accordance with the rest of the street, and she carried a shopping basket. This was a maid, or a housekeeper, going to do her shopping.

Dory was certain the maid that had initially opened the door to her and told her that Mr. Jones indeed lived there was younger. This woman was older. But now, Dory was torn about following this woman or staying to observe the door.

Technically, she could go ask this woman about Mr. Jones and she would have a corroborating story, but this was staff, and nothing happened within a house that other staff didn't know about. They would certainly know if relations were bad enough that a member of staff had murdered their employer. No, it felt wrong approaching this woman. If someone within the house had murdered the man, they had to be in on it together. There was no other way.

In saying that, Lady Wallisford had killed poor Nora Sands and no one had been the wiser. The point was that no one in the house had been complicit in hiding the murder. Dory's corroboration had to come from somewhere else. Perhaps a neighbor. The only way she would get that would be to knock on someone's door.

The housekeeper walked down the street, wearing her tweed jacket and sensible shoes. Nothing showy about this woman. The kind of person you would scarcely notice. Dory had to admit that she could hardly imagine the woman murdering anyone, but this was not about Dory's assumptions. Assumptions led to wrong answers.

A man appeared, holding a briefcase and Dory decided this was the person she would approach. "Excuse me," she called.

The man stopped and regarded her as she approached across the street.

"I am wondering if you know Mr. Jones. I believe he lives hereabouts."

"Yes," the man said, turning to consider the houses. "That one, number... sixteen, I believe."

"Do you know him?"

"Not well. We've met, of course. My wife knew his late wife. Widower."

"Oh, I am sorry to hear that." At this point, the man became curious about her motive. She could see it in his eyes. "My mother in law knew them a long time ago and I was just delivering a letter."

"Oh, I see," the man said, clearly believing her. "Well, number sixteen."

She really was becoming an accomplished liar. Perhaps not something to be proud of, but it was useful. Unlike Ridley, who couldn't really hide who he was and what he needed, she could be more stealthy.

"Have you seen him lately?" Dory asked. "I understand they were a very handsome couple. At least when my mother-in-law knew them."

"Well, I suppose they were a handsome couple. He became much more quiet after his wife died."

"Have you seen him lately?" Dory pushed.

"Uhmm," the man said, distracted by the question, rather than Dory's pushiness. "It's probably been a while now that I come to think of it."

This registered with Dory more than the man probably expected. "I thought I would knock on his door, but I'm afraid he might have left for work. I only have half a day. Do you know where I could find him if he's not at home?"

"He works at Pollack and Altman Insurers right next to Monument station."

"I should seek him there," Dory said. "Give him a chance to send a note back to Doris."

"Of course," the man said and gave a nod before continuing his walk.

She really was an accomplished liar, although she didn't think it was a skill her mother would be proud of. Lady Pettifer would be more enthusiastic about this revelation. Her lies had gained her much, though. She now knew where he worked and that he hadn't been seen for a while by at least one of his neighbors. The house was clearly occupied as the housekeeper went shopping in the morning. This wasn't the kind of neighborhood where there would be a second house in the country, like in some parts of London. This was likely the one and only residence of Mr Jones.

That was all well and good, but the simplest thing would be to knock on the door and ask for Mr. Jones. It could well be that he would come to the door and introduce himself. All this subterfuge might be for nothing.

Dory did just that and the same maid as before answered the door. "I'm sorry, Mr. Jones is not here," she said. "Would you like to leave a message? I can pass it on. He is a very busy man and also highly private, so sending requests through the mail might be the best option."

"Oh, of course," Dory said, feeling like an intruder. She smiled as the maid closed the door and then turned. The feeling of being intrusive followed her down the stairs back to the street, but then the doubts started to surface. Maybe she should have stressed how important it was to see him, but the young woman had said he was not there, which meant he must have left very early for work, before Dory got there shortly after the crack of dawn.

Chapter 22

WAKING IN THE AFTERNOON, Dory felt groggy, but also excited. Her inquiries that morning had made her even more suspicious. There was something wrong and she felt it in her bones, but she couldn't exactly put her finger on what.

Dressing and washing, she made her way downstairs to the kitchen, where Vera was eating a boiled egg with toasted bread cut into pieces.

"Fruitful morning?" Vera said, looking up from her breakfast. "I can see that by your eyes."

Dory sat down at the table. "There was something not right about the house next to the river, on Byron Street. I don't know what, but something was off. I'm off to his place of employment now to see if he's there. He could be and I could be completely wrong about all this, and then I'll be back to square one. The neighbor said Mr. Jones hadn't been seen for a while."

"That doesn't necessarily mean anything suspicious," said Vera. "We don't really notice our neighbors all the time, do we? It could simply be that this man hadn't seen him for a while."

Dory had to admit this was true, but she wouldn't know if her feeling was correct until she went to his place of employment, somewhere near Monument, which was, unfortunately, quite far away and it would take her at least an hour to get there, if not more. "I better go if I'm to be back by tonight."

"Don't be late," Vera said sternly. "Although I think we're going to have another clear night tonight."

Dory chewed her lip. There was a chance she might not get back in time. "Could you bring that extra blanket from my bed when you go? I don't want to cart it over half of London."

With a sigh, Vera gave Dory a chiding look. "Fine, but you owe me some manual labor in return. Betsy wants us to help in her mother's garden."

With a smile, and stealing a sliver of Vera's toast, Dory made her way out of the house and ran down the street towards the bus station. It took ten minutes before the bus heading west came along and she hopped on the back, handing over a shilling to the conductor.

The bus was quite unoccupied this time of day. Dory took a seat and watched the city go by as they drove westward. Most of the people coming on board were women and children with their shopping. Everyone seemed a little brighter for the quiet nights where most had slept in their own beds. It seemed such a luxury these days.

The busy streets around Monument were initially confusing when Dory got off the bus. It was an intersection of several streets and the great, big spire pierced the sky. Turning around, Dory searched for the insurer where Mr. Jones apparently worked. There were no visible signs on buildings so it was hard to find, leaving her to look inside quite a few buildings before she found the offices of Pollock and Altman on the second floor of the beige stone building with columns along the facade.

A staircase led her up and her footsteps steps echoed off the walls, until she reached the door with gold lettering on the glass, stating the name of Pollock and Altman Insurers.

The door led to the quiet office, decorated in dark wooden paneling, giving it a somber feel. A young man in a suit sat at a desk, and behind him were three clocks set at different times and a black Bakelite telephone right next to him.

"May I help you?" the young man said, looking down his nose at her even from a sitting position. Quite a feat. He must be well practiced.

"I was hoping to see Mr. Jones," Dory replied.

The young man's eyebrows rose. "I'm afraid he doesn't work here anymore," and it was Dory's turn to look surprised.

"Oh," she said, not quite knowing what to say now. "I had been told he works here. Has it been long since he left?"

"He retired about a year ago. He does drop in quite often. One of those who can't quite let go. He's still good friends with Mr. Pollock."

"Do you recall the last time he was here? I'm with the ATS, and we're doing a wellness check," she said with her most innocent-looking smile. "I'm having a bit of trouble reaching him, you see." The young man considered her and then picked up the receiver of the telephone. "Let me try calling," he said and spoke to the operator. He gave Mr. Jones' number, which apparently he knew by heart and the operator connected him forward. Dory could hear the subsequent ringing. "Hello this is Mr. Jones' residence," a young woman said. "How may I help you?

"This is Mr. Stevens from Pollock and Altman. May I speak to Mr. Jones, please?"

Dory didn't hear the rest of what was said as only mumbling reached her ears, but Mr. Stevens face remained impassive throughout, even as he hung up the receiver.

"It seems Mr. Jones is not at home," he said.

"Is that unusual?" Dory asked. "Does he leave London often?"

"No, never. He could simply be out."

"Yes, of course. When was the last time you heard from him in any capacity?" Dory asked

"Well, I sent him a bank draft about two weeks ago," he said, checking a book in front of him.

"But you didn't actually hear from him?"

There was a frown on the young man's face now and he was concerned. "I suppose it's been longer than that since I've actually seen or heard from him. Do you think something's happened to him? He has staff. Surely they will let us know if something untoward has happened. You don't think his house was bombed, do you? He lives in Limehouse."

"The house is intact, but he seems unavailable when I call. I'm not saying anything is wrong," Dory said with a smile. "It is just a wellness check—necessary in times like these. It could be that he is simply hard to reach. I will go and check at his house again. I'm sure there's nothing wrong. I will have him get in touch when I see him."

In truth, she didn't feel as confident as she tried to sound, but there was no point spreading panic. Ridley had taught her that. It was an irresponsible thing to spread panic when there was no real evidence for concern. "I'm sure everything is fine," Dory repeated. "And he will be in touch in a few days. Before I go, though, could you please ask if anyone in the office has seen him? It would be useful to know if someone else has heard from him in the last two weeks."

"Of course," the young men said, rising sharply and disappearing behind a dark wooden door, leaving Dory on her own in what really was a dark and gloomy room. She wouldn't like to spend the entire day in there like that young man seemed to do. The clocks on the wall ticked as she waited, disturbingly not in unison. It took a few moments, but the young man eventually returned. "It seems he came to dinner at Mr. Altman's house about a month ago."

"I see," Dory said and smiled again, trying to be reassuring. "Often people leave town with the recent bombardment we've had. It could well be that he's gone to stay with some distant relation."

The look on the young man's face wasn't convinced and that was concerning. If the people who knew him the most considered it unlikely he would leave town to go stay with relations, then maybe it was unlikely that he had. This visit to Mr. Jones' workplace certainly hadn't alleviated her concerns. There was something definitely off about all this. It was the same feeling she'd had about Baron Drecsay in Nice. Something was off, but she didn't know why.

With a farewell, Dory left the office and walked down the noisy stairs to the street below. Did she have enough evidence to go to the police? What could she tell them? That the people at the company he was retired from hadn't seen him for a while? That was hardly convincing. She needed to know more, needed something more concrete.

What she needed to do was go back and insist on seeing Mr. Jones, perhaps make an appointment for when they could meet. She had to think up some excuse. It would hardly do to tell the maids that he was suspected of being murdered. Well, if it came down to it, maybe she needed to fess up about why she was there. It could be that this was something they all laughed about when Mr. Jones made an appearance.

She would have to go back again tomorrow and talk to the maid, perhaps the housekeeper and relay that there were concerns about him not being seen. If that didn't succeed, she didn't know what to do.

Chapter 23

THE NEXT MORNING, Dory was in front of Mr. Jones' house as soon as she could be. It was barely past dawn and none of the men along the row of houses had come out for their morning commute yet.

It was so cold there was even ice floating on the blackness of the river. Dory's hands were shoved inside her jacket and her breath condensed. If she hadn't been in such a hurry, she would have had a cup of soup, but she wanted to be there at the earliest opportunity.

Slowly, the sun started to rise, and the biting cold started to alleviate. Dory kept watch as men slowly started to emerge, bracing themselves against the brisk morning. All the while, no one came out of Mr. Jones' house, although she saw when the staff drew back the curtains.

Being retired, she didn't expect Mr. Jones to come out like the other men heading to work, but the maid hadn't said he was away either. The first time she'd come, the maid had eluded he was in the house, the second, he'd been out—which both could be true. On the surface, there was nothing out of the ordinary—just a feeling that sat in the pit of her stomach.

When an hour had passed, she decided it wasn't worth waiting anymore. It was too early to call, but she could insist. Most pensioners she knew rose early.

Marching across the street, Dory used the brass doorknocker and waited. Finally, the young maid came to the door and smiled tightly. "Hello," she said.

Dory smiled in return. "I need to see Mr. Jones."

"He is unavailable," the young lady said and was about to close the door.

"I'm afraid it is necessary."

The girl didn't seem to know what to do. She was perhaps around eighteen, with a white maid's cap on her head.

"We are doing a wellness check on Mr. Jones. I am from the ATS."

"Please wait," the girl said and almost closed the door. Dory could hear whispers behind the door before it opened again, and the older woman stood there, the housekeeper. A slim woman with a narrow face, the constant disapproval of a housekeeper etched into the lines on her face. "I am sorry, Mr. Jones' is unavailable," the woman said sternly.

"There have been some concerns raised," Dory said.

"I can assure you that there is no need for concern, but Mr. Jones is unavailable to all visitors." With that, she firmly closed the door. Dory tried knocking again, but the door remained resolutely shut. The net curtains twitched at one point, but they were otherwise ignoring her.

Walking the steps, Dory looked up at the façade of the house. It had three stories, what had to be Mr. Jones' rooms on the second floor and the staff quarters on the third. There was nothing to be seen from the outside of the house. All looked still and calm.

At this point, Dory didn't know what to do. She couldn't very well barge through the door. For one, they weren't opening it for her, and she wasn't strong enough. Secondarily, she didn't really have a mandate to do so. The ATS did not do wellness checks on the elderly in the area. There was only so far she could take this ruse. And the police? Was it so uncommon that staff were given instructions to bar intruders? Not really. If Lord Wallisford did it, no one would bat an eyelid. Mr. Jones wasn't Lord Wallisford, but he was within his right to ask for privacy.

The concern for him was real, though. Mr. Stevens from Pollock and Altman was concerned. Perhaps the staff would be more amenable to letting Mr. Stevens in, but then they hadn't been all that forthcoming on the telephone the previous day.

With her hands on her hips, Dory tried to think of what to do. With this one, she had run out of options. She had to go to the police. Hopefully, the concern of Pollock and Altman would be enough to drive them to concern for Mr. Jones' wellbeing. Dory didn't know if this was enough. On the surface it really wasn't.

*

The Limehouse police station was a square brick building with a large archway in front from the time horses and carriages were used. The inside was painted a light green and a desk sergeant stood in a dark uniform.

Dory hadn't actually been in a police station since she had been called to divulge everything she knew about Baron Drecsay and his demise.

The large man with a red beard looked up, eyeing her as she walked in. Nerves welled up in her stomach and she didn't quite know what to say. The man said nothing as she approached. "I have concerns about one of your residents," she said. Could she go into the whole story behind her concerns, or get away without mentioning it. They would likely be just as receptive to her meddling as Captain Ridley was. "It seems no one has seen this man for quite some weeks, and his staff keep saying he is unavailable."

The sergeant considered her for a moment. He was a really imposing man. Perhaps that was a good trait in a desk sergeant, Dory wondered.

"And who is this man?"

"Mr. Jones of number sixteen Byron Street."

"Could simply be that the man likes his privacy."

"I told his staff there were concerns and I was there doing a wellfare check."

The man's eyes were piercing and Dory looked away. "And now you come to us?"

"And now I have done what I can, and must beseech you to see if this man is alive and well."

Reluctantly grabbing a piece of paper, he scribbled on it. "I'll speak to one of the bobbies and have him knock on the door."

Relief washed over Dory and she smiled. "Wonderful."

"Since when do the ATS run around and make wellfare checks?"

"Only when concern has been raised."

"How?"

Dory thought for a moment about how to say it. "In relation to some unaccounted for victims over in Poplar," she finally admitted. The man's eyebrows rose and Dory shrugged. It was the truth. Nothing more could be said. "If he is alive and well, then we'll know it wasn't him. If you need me, send a note to my address." Grabbing another piece of paper, he wrote down her address.

"Not to the ATS, then?" the man asked.

"The chances are less that it will reach me in a timely fashion." Dory looked up into his eyes and knew he understood that this had nothing to do with official ATS business. "We all owe it to the families to do our best to identify victims," she said.

"Aye," he agreed and put the note to side. "Not really an ATS job, though."

"Seems a job no one has time for." His eyebrows rose as if she'd just insulted him, and maybe she just had.

"We'll send you a note if anything comes of it."

That wasn't perhaps as assuring as she'd hoped. What she wanted was for him to say they would rush over there and barge in right then and there. But to this man, it was a low priority. It would perhaps be left to whichever bobby was responsible for that street. And everyone knew they were notoriously short-staffed at the moment. People literally got away with murder.

"Thank you, I would much appreciate it."

With that, she left, feeling the sergeant's eyes on her back. In her experience, policemen could be tricky when you were looking into something that was technically their job. Short-staffed and stretched thin, they still thought they were being imposed on if one tried to help. Even Ridley, when she had first met him had discouraged her, until it had gotten to the point where he was being frozen out.

Returning home, Dory went to bed. She was going to shortchange herself a little on sleep, but that couldn't be helped. Hopefully, the police had the matter in hand, so in a sense, she slept well.

Dropping her heavy boots on the floor by her bed, her feet ached and she remembered that she hadn't eaten anything. Her stomach gnawed with hunger, but she was too tired to go downstairs and eat. Besides, no one had gone to the store, so there was probably nothing down in the kitchen.

Would Ridley be proud of her now? Perhaps she would write to him and say she had finally handed the matter over to the police.

*

Her hopes were dashed, though, because no note came the next day, or the day after that. For once, Dory had time on her hands, sitting in their damaged kitchen, waiting for a note to be sent from the police.

"Perhaps you need to go check to see what happened," Vera suggested. "They could have misplaced your address. Or simply forgotten to tell you."

"Or they didn't go check on Mr. Jones at all," Betsy said. "They can be lazy those coppers, let me tell you. Good for nothing most of the time. Now get up. Mother wants that greenhouse raised."

They all knew that Betsy's brother had been scavenging glass panes from all over the area. Not that Dory could blame them. A long winter stretched before them and any vegetables they could grow would help feed the family.

Dory also didn't want to write to Lady Pettifer and admit that the police had simply ignored her, which is what she suspected had happened. It was embarrassing. Perhaps even more so if Lady Pettifer decided to ask her friend, the mother of the Commissioner of Police, to inquire. Lady Pettifer tended to be a broadsword when a scalpel was needed, but she was like that. They dealt with things on their own level, which was grossly out of line with the things Dory needed. It would be like setting off a bomb to kill a fly. As well-meaning as Lady Pettifer was, she didn't always understand nuance.

Equally, she didn't want to write to Ridley and say that she had been ignored, because he would probably say there wasn't sufficient cause for concern. A man not in his house when London was being bombed every night was hard to justify as the prelude to a crime.

Chapter 24

"MAIL CAME EARLY," Betsy said as they got home the next morning. It had been another clear night, and they had frozen stiff on the roof. "Looks like it's from your brother. Tom it says on the back."

"What?" Her brother Tom didn't write to her. He was only eight.

Dory took the letter. Sure enough, it was the uneven writing of an eight-year-old, the stamp crooked. Dory smiled at the sight of it. What was Tom doing writing her?

Shoving her finger in through the fold, she ripped it open and read. It talked about the rabbit he had.

Oh and mum broke her arm and is in hospital.

"What?" Dory said out loud.

"What's the matter?"

"My mother broke her arm."

"How?"

Dory turned the letter over, but there was nothing else. "It doesn't say."

"Is she alright?"

Well, how was Dory supposed to know that, she thought ungenerously. They had no phone, so it wasn't as if she could call. The postmaster did, but if her mother had broken her arm, she might not be able to come to the phone. If… "I have to go see if she is alright."

Racing, her mind tried to think through the logistics. She would have to take the train from Liverpool Street Station. Checking her watch, she tried to see what time it was. "Bugger."

"Just go," Betsy said. "We'll find some way to cover for you if you're not back."

"If we're lucky, it will be a clear night and nothing will happen. Just go. Here, take a sandwich," Betsy said, handing over the sandwich she was just about to bite into.

"Alright," Dory said, her body still paralyzed with indecision. "Right. Bus."

"Yes, take the bus. Run along. Do you have any money?"

"Yes. Yes, I do," Dory said and pulled on the jacket she had just taken off. "Alright, I better go."

"I hope everything is fine. I'm sure it will be," one of the girls said as Dory opened the door and stepped outside. Automatically her feet took her toward the bus station. What if her mum wasn't alright? What then? Dory tried to think through the implications. Harry was off in the mines, and Tom would need somewhere to go. Either Dory had to quit the ATS, or Tom would have to come to her, and stay here in the East End where the Germans dropped bombs just about every night. That was not a good solution.

The bus was crowded when it came. It was just on midday and people were… Actually, Dory had no idea why so many people were on the bus this time of day. Slowly, the bus trundled along Whitechapel northward toward Barbican. It had been a while since Dory had been up this way. The bombing damage extended all this way. It was sad what this had done to the city.

The trip cost her one pound fifty, and she could probably only pay it because Lady Pettifer had given her money. But ticket in hand, she waited on the platform for the train to come. The porters were all women, which Dory hadn't noticed before. But there were still men in dark suits with their whistles, directing trains and traffic. The trains had to keep running. They were the lifeline of the country.

Dory wondered if any of the lines had been bombed. Surely the Germans were trying to strike them. Not that the BBC would report it if any of them were struck.

Finally, the dark mass of the locomotive came, steam billowing along the roof of the station as it came to the platform. Dory found a seat next to an elderly woman with a large package tied with string. The woman smiled and Dory returned it.

Now that she was sitting and the shock of the news was wearing off, Dory couldn't keep her eyes open.

"Where are you going, dear?" the woman asked.

Groggily, Dory opened her eyes. "Sorry, just got off duty. Swanley."

"You get some kip and I'll keep an eye out for your station."

"They've taken the station names down," Dory stated.

"In my years, I have done this journey a hundred times. I live in Dover."

"That must be interesting," Dory mumbled, genuinely interested in what life was like in Dover in these times, but her body wouldn't keep up with her curiosity, so she slept.

"Here you go," said the woman touching her on the knee. It felt as though Dory had just closed her eyes in London and woken the next moment in Swanley. "Hurry now."

"Thank you," Dory mumbled, her knees feeling unsteady as she stood, walking with a woolly mind down toward the car door. "Hello, Mr. Mitchell," she said as she saw the old stationmaster.

"Dory, how are you?" he said. "Haven't seen you back here in ages."

"It's been ages." Dory blinked, trying to clear her head. "Mum's injured."

"So I hear."

Mr. Mitchell blew his whistle and it pierced Dory's ear. The train blew its whistle and started chugging away. "Thought I would check on her."

"I'm sure she will appreciate it." His calm words reassured her. Mr. Michell was always calm and collected. Things would be alright. Mum would be fine, Dory said, but she felt the nervousness reassert itself.

"Bye, then."

"Bye, Dory," the stationmaster said and walked toward the station. "Give my regards to your mother and let me know if she needs anything. Beatrice will be more than happy to help."

With a nod, Dory ran to the station exit and down the street, seeing the familiar brick buildings she had grown up around. Her mother's house wasn't far away and Dory ran the whole way, reaching the small terrace home where she had been born.

"Mum," she said, walking in the door.

"Dory," Tom said, appearing in the small entrance. "You're here."

"Where's Mum?"

"Upstairs in bed."

"Is she alright? Are you alright?"

"Mum's got a gypsum cast."

"Yeah?" Dory said. "You told me in your letter that she broke her arm. I'm going to go up and see her now."

"Okay," Tom said in the nonplussed way of an eight-year-old.

Dory walked up the staircase, the third step creaking like it always did. Her mother's door was open and Dory found her lying in bed, her arm in a sling. "Mum."

"Dory. What are you doing here?"

"Tom wrote and said you'd broken your arm," Dory said and walked over to the bed to sit down. Her mother's room smelled so familiar and comforting, but her mum groaned when Dory sat down. "Is it sore?"

"It throbs like you wouldn't believe."

"What happened?"

"Well, there's this motor at the cannery and if you're not quick enough, the starter crank can whip around and take your arm off, which it did in this case. Broke my arm in two places. Quite clean breaks, they say, so that's something."

"I'm sorry. Are you alright?"

"You didn't have to come."

"Tom said you were in hospital."

"Well, they let me out. I'm fine, love. No need to worry. It will be six weeks before it will come right. Financially, it is not ideal."

"I can give you some money."

"You don't have to."

"It's not a problem. I have enough to help."

Her mum smiled. "I heard you saw Gladys not so long ago. How is she?"

"Good. Obviously she has to work harder now that the house has barely any help, but she's happy enough. They have plenty of food."

"More chicken than they know what to do with. She's sending us one for Christmas. A live one."

"Can they do that?"

"Apparently. Are you coming home for Christmas?"

"I don't think so. Not sure the Nazis celebrate Christmas. They would be spiteful enough not to."

"I worry for you so much. How are things in London?"

"Messy, but people get on with their business. Not much else you can do, really," Dory said and crossed her legs. Now that she was with her mother, it seemed like no time had passed at all.

"Grant's David asked about you the other day?" David was a boy Dory had gone to school with. Probably not a boy anymore. Apparently he'd been excused from the draft. There were all sorts of reasons that people were excused.

"I can't stay long," Dory said. "I have to get back."

"Just a flying visit, then?"

"Are you sure you're alright? Maybe I can stay a couple of hours," Dory said, guilt welling up in her. The clouds were gathering outside and the Germans would come. Still, Dory was probably going to be late for the start of her shift anyway. The four thirty train would be fine. "I'm investigating a murder."

"Are you still getting involved with such silliness."

Dory lay down along the foot of her mother's bed, but rose again as the softness of the bed was too tempting.

"I don't know who is putting all these silly ideas in your head. Gladys told me about some detective."

A blush crept up Dory's cheeks at the mention of Ridley. He was not someone she was ready to talk to her mother about.

"There is always need for more hands at the cannery. You can always come back home."

"I'm needed where I am."

"But it's so dangerous."

"It is necessary. We must all do what is necessary."

"Well, you running around and playing detective is not necessary, Dory. It's unseemly."

Apparently the police thought so too, because there wasn't a peep from them.

"No one cares about seemly anymore, Mum. You lying in bed with a broken arm is unseemly."

Her mother sighed. "Be a darling and cook us supper before you go. My arm will apparently stop throbbing in a few days."

"I'll do a big stew that will last a few days."

"You're going to have to go to the shop, because we're out of just about everything. Tom is starting to eat like his brother—anything he can get his hands on."

"I'll take him to the shop with me. Maybe there will be some treat we can get."

"That would be the day," her mother said, and raised the magazine she was reading.

Chapter 25

DORY ARRIVED AT Liverpool Street Station after dark. They'd had to cover all the windows of the train at dusk, which created a very claustrophobic environment within the car, so it was nice to step out into the dark skies. Unfortunately, it was raining, but Dory was still glad to escape as she ran for the bus heading to Poplar.

There hadn't been an air raid yet, so the bus was still running. Otherwise, she would have a long walk. But her luck didn't hold. On Whitechapel high street, the familiar wail of the sirens started and the bus pulled over at the nearest shelter and the few passengers were urged out.

For Dory, though, she needed to get over to Poplar and started running down the emptying streets. A warden stopped her and she had to shout 'ATS' without slowing down.

Before long, the rumble of the planes came, then the whine of the dropping bombs. In the sky, the parachutes of the different bombs were also seen. Seems the Germans were carrying mixed loads that night. An incendiary even landed down in front of her, looking like a long baton, exploding into showers of sparks when it landed. They were filled with flammable oil that flared.

It had landed next to a cloth merchant and the building would start burning in a minute. Dory was torn between keeping going and finding some means for dealing with this bomb. They were so damned bright, they burned the eyes, but she stopped running and went in search of a sandbag, which never seemed to be around when needed.

A few doors down, she found one and hauled it back, throwing it on where she assumed the bomb was amidst the bright sparks. The sparks burned the bare skin of her hands and she probably had little burn marks all over her trousers as well. It didn't take, so she had to go back for a second one, which did manage to quell the bomb, but the fire had spread up the wood paneling of the shop.

Finding an empty, she beat the flames, hearing the bomb trying to burn its way through the sand. The rain would get it before it did any more damage. That shop was lucky she was passing. It survived to trade another day.

Putting this bit of excitement behind her, she started running again. Fires had started elsewhere and the whine of the fire engine could be heard coming down the street. Dory had to ignore those. They were too established for her to help. She had to get to her post.

Arriving at Poplar, she could see the searchlight traveling across the sky. They had managed to get it working, but Vera was likely manning it, which meant she couldn't do any spotting. They were basically working blind.

Another wave of planes came overhead and the familiar whine followed. These were dropping nearby. Dory felt it in her bones and her concern grew into panic. They couldn't be seen, only heard, and this one was coming closer and closer. She didn't know what to do. Was she standing in the wrong place, or running to the wrong place. It was all a gamble, but this one would hit.

A shower of brightness slammed into her eyes, or was that the percussion of the bomb. It was too bright to tell where it was, but she wasn't knocked to the ground. It couldn't have been that close, but it was definitely in front of her. The searchlight. They had been targeting the searchlight, Dory realized.

The brightness receded to darkness, but that might simply be her eyes. She couldn't run for a moment, because she couldn't see. The bright lights were burned into her eyes and blinking didn't shift the glowing hindering her sight. A sense of panic pierced through her. They had struck the searchlight.

Blinking furiously, she tried to clear her vision, which she could manage in the peripheries of her vision. Vera and Betsy were up there. They had been struck. Cloying panic reasserted itself. This could not be happening.

Eventually, her vision cleared somewhat. There were still red spots in the center of her vision, but she could move, slowly walking toward the building they used. The bell of the fire engine was heard, and as Dory got closer, she could see it was the building next door that had been struck.

Relief flooded through her. Hopefully there hadn't been anyone in that building. Rushing forward into her building, she climbed the stairs three at a time.

Dory bypassed the radio room and went straight to the roof, her concern more for Vera. It was dark as she got to the roof. The searchlight had stopped working, and the only light was the glow from the dancing flames of the fire. The building next door cracked and groaned in its demise.

A lump was moving and Dory rushed forwards. "Vera?"

"WHAT?" Vera said and Dory helped her to stand, which she was having some trouble with.

"Are you alright?"

"WHAT? I CAN'T HEAR A DAMNED THING. THEY GOT US, I THINK."

"They got next door."

"WHAT? IS BETSY ALRIGHT?"

"I'll go check."

"KNOCKED ME CLEAR OFF MY FEET," Vera yelled as Dory ran back to the doorway to the stairs. Again taking three steps at a time until she got down to the radio room. It was utterly dark in there, but she saw Betsy's outline.

"The whole building shook. I thought it was going to collapse for a moment," Betsy said, taking her headphones off. "Is Vera alright?"

"Seems to be in one piece."

"Bloody hell. That was a close one."

"Next door," Dory confirmed.

"We heard it coming. It just got closer and closer. I've never been so scared. Completely cut the power. We're dead. The radio's dead."

"The searchlight is off too."

"The engineers will have to come look at it in the morning. There's nothing we can do. Might as well go home."

"YOU IN HERE?" Vera said from the doorway.

"We're here."

"STILL CAN'T HEAR A DAMNED THING. MY EARS ARE RINGING LIKE CHURCH BELLS."

"Let's go home. Are you alright? No cuts?"

"WHAT?"

Betsy moved forward and grabbed Vera by the arm, making walking movements with her fingers.

"SEARCHLIGHT IS DEAD."

"WE KNOW," Betsy shouted.

"We need to go in case the fire spreads," Dory said.

Both of them took Vera by the elbows as if she were an invalid, which annoyed her. They emerged to chaos outside. The fire brigade was there, pumping water onto the building where fire spilled out of the windows, the orange glow reflecting off every surface around. The heat was extraordinary.

Another wave of planes flew above them.

"BASTARDS," Vera yelled.

"Come, let's go," Dory said.

"We should probably go to a shelter," Betsy said. "But what are the chances that we'll get bombed twice in one night."

The last thing Dory wanted to do was to sit cramped like a sardine in a shelter which stunk of waste.

"How was your mum? I didn't think to ask," Betsy asked. Vera wasn't paying attention, which showed she still didn't hear anything. Hopefully it wouldn't be permanent.

"Broke her arm. She's at home resting. It will take six weeks to heal the doctors say."

"That's rotten," Betsy said. "She'll be alright, though?"

"Yeah. The neighbors will help her. Swanley is good that way."

The streets were dark and empty, except for the firefighters and the rescue brigade. It was a busy night, as if the Germans were catching up on what they missed during the clear nights.

"THAT SEARCHLIGHT IS BLOODY HOT," Vera shouted. "I'M STILL COOKING FROM IT."

"Any notes come from the coppers?" Dory asked. She knew that Betsy had a less than kind opinion of the police.

"Nope. Those bastards never do anything you actually need them to."

In this case, that seemed to be right.

"Well, I am glad you are both still alive," Dory said. "You had me worried there for a bit."

"You and me both," Betsy said. "That was scary. I thought without a doubt that Vera had copped it."

"WHAT?" Vera said.

"NOTHING. GLAD WE'RE STILL ALIVE."

"ME TOO," Vera said with a smile.

"Maybe we should go to the hospital and have her checked out?" Dory said.

"What for? What are they going to do other than tell us that her hearing is shot and they hope it recovers?"

That was true. There was little they could do.

A fire engine rushed passed them.

"Get to a shelter," a man with a warden helmet demanded.

"Oh, piss off," Betsy roared back. "We've already been bombed once tonight. Don't need you piping off at us."

Betsy had the means to be completely ineloquent when she felt like it, or when she was stressed.

"WE LEFT OUR SANDWICHES BEHIND," Vera yelled.

"Bugger," Betsy said. "We've got practically nothing at home. Maybe I can go around to Mum's and nick some bread."

"Or we'll go to the shelter and buy some Chelsea buns."

"It's so sad that we go to the shelter for food," Betsy stated, but it was the only place to buy food during the night. Usually they had quite a range. Apparently, some people made their living selling food in the shelters. "Fine, we'll go."

Chapter 26

FOR ONCE, DORY WOKE up feeling refreshed, perhaps because she'd slept close to twelve hours. They'd left the shelter shortly after midnight, when the bombing seemed to die down. The all-clear hadn't been blown, but they decided to risk it. Now it was close to midday when she got up to what looked like a fairly clear winter's day.

Her thoughts turned to Vera, who had been the most injured from last night, and then her mother. Then Ridley, her brothers, and even Vivian—all these people she had to worry about.

She was going to write Lady Pettifer later today, but she might go speak to the Limehouse police first, to see if they had actually done something and forgotten to inform her. After deliberation, she decided to omit how close the bomb had been last night. There would be no purpose in telling Lady Pettifer and it would only make her worry more. There was too much worry as it was in this war.

Vera was downstairs, spreading butter on a piece of bread.

"How are you?" Dory asked.

"My ears are still ringing, but I can hear now. I hope it stops, because it's driving me up the wall. I thought I would go over and see what the engineers say. I'm not actually sure they know about the damage yet."

"Maybe not. I don't know if the warden would have informed them. It's good that you're heading over. I am going to speak to the police."

"Going police wrangling?" Vera sat down and took a bite out of her slice of bread. "Betsy's gone around to her mum's. It's lucky you weren't there last night. You would have been the one who copped it." Which was true. Dory would maybe even have been closer to the blast than Vera had been.

"Yeah," she said with a nervous chuckle. Maybe if she hadn't stopped to fight that incendiary, she would have been on that roof. "And I saved a shop."

It was a statement Vera chose not to pursue. "Well, good luck with your sleuthing. I doubt we'll be on duty tonight. Probably not tomorrow either, but who knows. I suspect the transformer got blown to pieces."

"Most likely," Dory agreed. "I'll head out."
She'd get something to eat on the way. Maybe a pasty. That sounded nice. After last night, she wanted something filling and greasy.

Down on the high street, she decided to take the bus rather than walk. Some days you were simply better off not seeing the damage around you, and on the bus, she could ignore it. At times, she needed to ignore the war and the devastation, and to focus on other things. Besides, she needed to think what to do if the police refused to help. Maybe there was some other authority she could call on. It could be that the ATS would actually help if she asked them to. Or the warden. They had some rights to interfere, Dory believed. They seemed to think so anyway.

The door to the police station was open and Dory walked in seeing the same sergeant as before. "I'm here about the house on Byron Street," she said and smiled.

The man looked at her wearily. "Not sure your request has been gotten to," he admitted. "Not our highest priority, you understand."

"I think it needs to be. There is a good possibility that there is a crime involved. The body in question did not appear to be a victim of the raids."

The man eyed her, almost as if he suspected she was lying.

"Harley," he called, surprising her as his voice boomed. His attention turned to a man who was passing by. "This woman is concerned about a resident on your street. Byron Street."

"I haven't gotten to it."

Dory left the sergeant and approached this constable, who was apparently responsible for the beat covering Byron Street. "I am having difficulties locating this man, and his staff are not being helpful."

The young man sighed and Dory stared at him hopefully. Then he sighed again. "We can head over there now, if you wish."

"Perfect," Dory said. "It would be good to settle this."

The man walked out, putting on his round bobby's hat. "You mentioned something about a crime."

"Yes, a body was found on a bombing site, except, he had no indicators of being in the building when it went down. The doctor at the morgue said so. There was no identity on him, but by certain scars on his body, I was able to determine that it might be Mr. Jones. But I can't seem to get hold of him, and the staff at the firm where he is still quite involved, haven't seen him either. They send him bank drafts on a regular basis, so that would be motive, of course." Everything was pouring out of her.

The young man stared at her as if she were unhinged. "It is a matter for the police if it's true."

"Of course it's true," Dory said, offended. "But I had to bring something convincing to the police first, didn't I?"

This young man didn't like her, but that was fine. He was doing what she wanted, so he could dislike her all he wanted.

They approached the house and the young man marched straight up to the door and banged on it. "Police," he yelled.

"There is a maid and a housekeeper. They seem to be the only people in the house."

The door opened promptly and Dory looked up. It was the housekeeper and she stared daggers at

Dory before smiling sweetly to the policeman. "How may I help you?"

"We are here to speak to Mr. Jones. Is he here?"

"He is unavailable."

"Where is he?" the young man said, clearly very forceful in nature when he wanted to be. Dory was impressed.

"Upstairs, but he is indisposed."

The policeman pushed passed her and Dory followed.

"This is really uncalled for," the woman said, running after them. "Mr. Jones is unwell. He does not wish to receive visitors." There was an edge of desperation in her voice, which told Dory something was definitely up.

They walked on the carpeted stairs up to the second story. The staircase was a dark mahogany. The insurance business had obviously been very rewarding to Mr. Jones.

A double set of doors, seemed to lead to the master bedroom and Constable Harley headed right there. He banged on the door. "Police, we are coming in," he announced.

"Stop," the housekeeper demanded. "This is unjust."

It was a curious choice of words in Dory's mind, but she didn't have time to consider it further as Harley continued into the doors.

Frantic murmuring came from a disheveled figure in the bed and Dory's hopes were dashed. The room smelled of an unwashed body. But this wasn't the man who had been found on Pennyfield Street at all. He was obviously here. The murmuring sounded like help.

"What's the matter with him?" Harley demanded. The man was staring at Harley as if his life depended on it.

"He is unwell," the housekeeper said, much more calmly now. The maid had appeared behind her and there was fear in her eyes. These two were up to something. "As you can see. We really need to leave him to rest."

The man tried to speak, but it sounded garbled. His hair was messy and gray stubble covered his sunken cheeks. Lips were white and cracked. He looked awful. This was certainly not a man who had been groomed anytime lately. That he was unwell was clear to see.

"What is wrong with him?" Dory asked.

The man turned his attention to her. He was trying to reach for her. He clearly wanted help.

"He has fits," the woman said. "He is quite unwell."

"Is a doctor attending to him?"

"Of course."

The man viciously disagreed. He was pointing accusingly at the woman.

"He needs to go to the hospital," Dory said, trying to understand what was going on.

"There is nothing they can do according to the doctor."

"Liar," the man accused through his garbled speech.

"There is a telephone," Dory said. "I will call the ambulance. You better stay here." She had the feeling they should not leave Mr. Jones alone. There was a terrified, desperate look in his eyes.

The housekeeper's mouth had drawn so tight, it looked like a pouch drawn together.

"Where's the telephone?" Dory barked at the younger maid, who pointed downstairs.

"We didn't do anything," the girl said, which again indicated that they very much had done something.

Dory located the phone in the hallway and spoke to the operator, who agreed to send the ambulance over to the address.

Taking a moment, Dory tried to understand what was going on. A purse which looked new stood on the table in the entranceway—an unusual object for a widow, but then the widow was upstairs, confined to his bed. There was also a coat hanging over a chair, which was definitely not where staff should be leaving their things. Dory realized what was happening. His staff were receiving his bank drafts and had run over the house while the master was languishing upstairs, unable to move. They'd neglected to get him medical assistance so they could keep him as an invalid, and enjoyed living well beyond their means. If Dory cared to look, she was sure they had moved their belongings down into the bedrooms of the second story and had taken over the house.

By the time Dory had returned upstairs, the housekeeper and maid were handcuffed together. Constable Harley stood with his arms crossed, staring narrowly at them. The girl was sobbing and repeating that they hadn't done anything.

"The ambulance is on the way," Dory said quietly. There was definitely a crime here. It just wasn't her crime.

Chapter 27

DORY HAD A HEADACHE when she returned
home. The maid and the housekeeper were carted off
by the police, and Mr. Jones was taken by ambulance
to the Royal London Hospital. Breaking their way in
through that door had opened a hornet's nest that
Dory still couldn't wrap her head around.

The callousness was just beyond belief. To
simply ignore that man's suffering for a chance to live
in the comfort of his house and to spend his bank
draft. It was unfathomable.

On a level, she could understand that staff were
not always the greatest admirers of the people they
worked for. Dory had herself struggled to admire
quite a few of the people at Wallisford Hall, but she
would never stand by when one of them was
suffering. The truth was that she couldn't understand
crime. DI Ridley seemed more accepting that it
regularly happened, but it always took her by
surprise. It was a curious trait for someone as driven
to investigate as she was. Perhaps she wanted to
prove to herself that there was an innocent

explanation. How could she look at any of the people around her and expect that one of them would be so heartless as to take another person's life—and for such trivial reasons. She couldn't.

Sadly, in her quest to believe there were innocent reasons behind the bad things that happened, she was proven wrong most of the time.

The other truth was that Mr. Jones was not the man who had been found in Pennyfield Street. He could most certainly be crossed off the list. This left a few more to confirm, but it also meant she had to return to Mr. Dellow, who simply couldn't be reached.

On the way home, she detoured to his street and knocked on his door. Yet again, there was no answer and the house was dark inside. That didn't necessarily mean anything suspicious. There was no sign that the bombings wouldn't come that night. He could have retreated to an air shelter, or he could simply be staying elsewhere. There was nothing overtly suspicious.

As she reached her own street, the air raid sirens started whining. Picking up speed, she ran the rest of the way. Their house didn't have a basement, where many people set up their own shelters. There was nothing to protect them if a bomb fell.

Neither Vera nor Betsy were at home. Betsy was likely with her mum. Vera was probably out dancing, particularly if her boyfriend, Kevin, had the night off. As rarely as they got time off, Kevin would likely try to swing a free night to join her.

The school down the road had a public shelter in its basement, and after last night, she didn't want to tempt fate by staying out in the open. Making herself a sandwich, she packed it away into her bag and locked up the house.

Some people were running, while others calmly walked. The planes couldn't even be heard yet, so there wasn't the utmost urgency. The nearby railway arches were also shelters, but Dory walked to the school, which was closer.

'Air raid shelter' was painted on the wall with white paint, an arrow pointing to a set of stairs down the side of the building. Sandbags surrounded the entranceway and the side of the building. It was the first time Dory had been to this one. It had a musty smell. A single electric bulb hung in every room. The place was a series of small rooms.

By the look of it, it would likely have been some kind of storage area before, but now it was cleared out of everything but benches, mattresses and blankets.

"This way, to the back," a warden said, urging people to get out of the main thoroughfare. "Make room and settle down."

It took time to get through the main thoroughfare, which was a bottleneck for getting into the room. For a shelter, it didn't have the ideal design. Eventually Dory found herself in one of the rooms with about two dozen other people.

She spotted Mrs. Mellison, their neighbor, sitting on one of the benches, knitting something with yellow yarn.

Then the blasts started. People didn't even react. They were so used to it. There were blasts far away and ones closer. The close ones caused dust to dislodge from the beams above, but no one seemed to react to this either. They really should clean that dust off, so it didn't sprinkle on them every time there was a bomb close enough, but no one had bothered.

The walls were brick and the cold of the space soon warmed with the number of bodies in the room. The electric bulb flickered with one of the blasts and then extinguished leaving them utterly in the dark. Grumbles and groans spread through the gathered crowd until someone lit a lamp.

"Must have hit one of the transformers again," an elderly man said.

"Tea?" a woman said at the door, carrying four cups in her hands.

"Yes, please," a man said and reached a coin out to the woman, who gave him a cup in return.

"How much?" Dory asked.

"Sixpence," she replied and Dory pulled out her small leather purse and rifled through her coins until she found a sixpence. A cup of tea sounded like a lovely idea. "Any buns?"

"I'll send Florrie over this way," the woman said and took Dory's coin. The enamel cup was warm, the tea steaming hot.

Dory pulled out her notebook and shifted off the bench to sit on the floor, where she could use the bench as a writing desk. Between sips of the tea, she started composing a letter to Lady Pettifer, to inform her of the day's strange events.

Another blast shook the structure and Dory quickly covered her teacup with her palm to stop the dust from floating down into it. A baby started crying in the room next door. A nearby man was already snoring.

When she was done, people were starting to arrange mattresses, getting ready to bed down for the night. It was strange bedding down with lots of people who Dory barely knew. Most of the people around here seemed to know each other, but she'd only come into this neighborhood a few months back.

Florrie never came with the buns, so Dory had to make due with her sandwich, before accepting a spot on a mattress next to a young girl who looked about sixteen. It took some time to get to sleep. The sounds of other people snoring and shifting were something Dory wasn't used to. Well, not since she'd lived at home with her brothers. It felt a lifetime ago, even if it was only three years back.

As she closed her eyes, Dory's thoughts returned to Mr. Jones, and hoped he was alright.

Poor man had been trapped in his own body, knowing he had fallen prey to these women who cared nothing about his wellbeing. It was a scary thought, and it made her feel a little claustrophobic for a moment, before she told herself to get a grip on her panic.

Mr. Jones was free of his predicament and it was because of her. That was something to feel proud of. She'd made a monumental difference in someone's life. That had never happened to her before.

Now if she could just locate Mr. Dellow. He liked to spend time in the library, someone had said. Flipping over her notebook, she looked back at what she'd written. That would be her plan for tomorrow, to check for him in the library, perhaps talk to the staff if he wasn't there.

Another bomb shook the building. Seething anger rose in Dory. When was this going to stop? It was that anger that made them so stubborn that they refused to relent to it. They certainly weren't going to cower. Sadly, they heard so little about what was happening with the war. It felt a little like they weren't trusted with that knowledge. Hopefully that was because of spies rather than the idea that things weren't going well.

A dog barked somewhere in the shelter. Someone had brought their dog with them, which was perhaps understandable.

It was a heavy night of bombing that night and Dory was glad she had chosen to come here. It wasn't comfortable, but she wouldn't be sleeping much in her own bed that night either. Didn't seem to bother some, who snored uninterrupted all night, lying in the uncomfortable closeness of other sleeping bodies, and the faint smell of urine from the latrine. There wasn't much dignity in this, but they had to make do. They would make do—out of sheer spite.

Perhaps it was that same stubbornness with which she refused to give up on her investigation into the man found of Pennyfield Street. People who did horrible things had to be stood up to and defied.

Chapter 28

LOOKING UP, DORY took in the Victorian brick building that was the Watney Market library. It was a pleasant surprise to find it intact. It wasn't something that could be taken for granted these days.

Inside were wooden shelves and old, bound books. It wasn't large, but it had a decent enough selection. Dory looked longingly at the books. How long had it been since she'd read a book? There simply wasn't the time to lay in bed and read. And sadly, she didn't suspect there would be time until this infernal war was over.

A creak stole her attention away and she saw an elderly man dressed a little out of fashion, dressed in a dark suit with a fob watch, standing behind the issuance desk. "Excuse me," Dory said as she approached and the man slowly looked up. "I am looking for Mr. Frank Dellow. I believe he visits here quite often."

"Comes to read the paper," the man said.

Looking around, Dory tried to see anyone doing so, or even where one would do so. "He's not here by any chance?"

"No, he's not. He hasn't been in quite some time. I've grown quite worried for him. I hope he hasn't met with misfortune. One of those who refuses to shelter in the evenings."

"His house is still intact. I was there yesterday, but I haven't been able to find him. Do you know where he might be?"

"Can't pretend I knew him that well. He came here most days. Reads the paper. I would have no idea beyond that what he does with himself."

"Which really means I have gotten no further. He doesn't work anywhere?" That wasn't entirely true, because she now knew that he wasn't doing his usual routine and there was someone worried about him. It was the first real piece of evidence that something was not right with Mr. Dellow.

"No, he was on a pension." In light of what had happened to Mr. Jones, her initial fear was that someone was trying to steal his pension, but that was nothing but an unfounded accusation. Still, it had to be considered. Money was an undeniable motive for murder.

"Did he have any relations?"

"I don't believe so. He seemed a very solitary man. A widower. There was a daughter, but she died in childbirth some years back." Turns out this man knew quite a bit about Mr. Dellow's background.

"And he was interested in the news?" she asked, concluding so if he religiously read the papers. Not everyone was interested in the news about the world outside of their community.

"Of course he was," the man stated sharply. "Our country is at war, in case you hadn't noticed."

"Believe me, I have. Anything in particular related to the war he was interested in?"

"Just generally. Some people like to keep themselves informed. Of late, though, he was interested in the municipal organization related to the war. He felt some things were managed poorly." Many would say that was an understatement.

"Anything in particular?"

"Not that he mentioned."

With that, the man gave a shrug and walked away. There was nothing else here for her, Dory concluded, so she walked outside and found a bench. The cold of it seeped through her clothes, but she wanted to record what she had just learnt in her notebook, and it was summed up as: *on a pension, liked reading the papers, and complained about municipal organization.*

That described just about every sixty-year-old man in the country. It was nothing to go on. In fact, she had nothing to go on at all. Back to square one.

This sleuthing thing wasn't always easy or simple. Sometimes there was just nothing, and it was incredibly frustrating.

Perhaps she could speak to the warden. It was the only thing she could think of, and also wait until this evening and knock on the doors of the neighbors before the air siren wailed. They would perhaps know something more, maybe something that would eliminate him as the body found.

For once she had time on her hands and nothing to do. There really wasn't much to do. She didn't really have any friends here, and they would all be working besides. The shops were just about bare and the museums were all closed. Maybe she should return home and read a book like she always wished she could. Now was her chance—she'd just gotten out of the habit.

Determining to do so, she walked home, finding Betsy and Vera huddled over the stove. "Okay, slowly," Betsy said.

"What are you doing?" Dory asked, walking into the kitchen, giving a wave to Mrs. Mellison through the hole in the wall.

"Making lipstick. Mum had this old beeswax candle, so we're making lipstick."

"Kevin found a small pot of glycerin," Vera continued. "It's looking really good." There were barrels of glycerin at the munitions factory Dory had worked at.

"What are you using for color?"

"Beetroots. We squeezed the life out of a couple of them, and it's making quite a nice color. My friend Sally said she used charcoal and made a serviceable mascara. Thought we'd try it after. God knows there's enough charcoal around."

"Good idea," Dory said a little unconvinced, but what was the harm in trying? The girls both shifted over from the stove to huddling over the bench as they poured out the concoction they'd just made.

"It's actually a really nice color."

"Hot, hot," Betsy said. "How'd the sleuthing go?"

"Nowhere. I've got to find some of the neighbors to talk to, but they're not home during the day and I'll likely only have a few minutes before they all rush off to the shelter."

"So go talk to them at the shelter," Vera said, making it sound like the most natural conclusion. Why hadn't Dory thought of that? Of course, she would have a captive audience all night. Most of them would go to the same shelter. Granted, she didn't yet know where, but that was something she could find out.

"That is brilliant," Dory finally admitted. "I guess I am spending the night there."

"Me and Kevin are going dancing."

"Now there is a surprise," Dory said flatly.

"Only for an hour, though, as he has to start a shift. Couldn't get a second night off. I think he's going to propose soon. He'd better. I'm not hanging on as some goodtime girl. Come the start of next year, I want a ring on my finger."

"I'm sure he will," Betsy assured.

"I am going to go upstairs and read," Dory said, to the surprised expressions of the girls. They weren't readers at the best of times, whereas Dory wanted to escape somewhere where there wasn't a war. Maybe she would re-read that old gothic novel she had about a Governess stuck with a remote family out on the moors. She loved that book and could happily immerse herself in that world for a while, where monsters turned out to be shadows, and not flying machines made in Germany.

Lying down on her bed, she pulled her blanket over her and picked up the book lying on the bottom shelf of her nightstand. It had dust on it, so it had been a while.

The next moment she looked up, the colors of dusk were painted all over the sky. Hours had passed and she hadn't noticed. In a rush, she threw the blanket off herself and rushed downstairs. Both Vera and Betsy were gone and the house was darkening. Grabbing her bag, she left and ran toward Mr. Dellow's area.

In the end, she simply followed a woman and a toddler to a shelter, where people from the neighborhood streamed into one large room in the basement of a factory. The people in the factory were mandated to work throughout the raids. Dory wasn't sure what they produced, but it was clearly vital.

Dory looked around. There had to be close to two hundred people in there, and not a single face she recognized. The shuffling to get positioned died down. There were a few resourceful people who hung hammocks between pipes running along the walls, while most people had blankets or cots on the floor, amiably chatting. The place smelled like oil and metal, but it wasn't nearly as claustrophobic as the last one she had been in.

Clearly she wasn't as prepared as some, who brought their entire family supper with them. Or bringing suitcases with clothes, books and other entertainments. One man had even brought a record player and the dulcet tones of a trumpet echoed through the place, drowning out the drone of the machinery above their heads.

It felt a little like intruding, going to an unknown shelter.

"Find a seat, girl," a man said and Dory sat down at the nearest vacant spot.

"Do you know Frank Dellow?" she asked the man. "I was looking for him when the siren went off. He's on Hurst Street."

"Can't say that I do. New to the area."

Why was it that the people new to the area that were the most helpful?

"I think Mrs. Simpson lives near Hurst Street, though. There's no person around here she don't know about," he said and she blinked at him for a moment until he remembered to point the woman out.

Dory nodded gratefully and shifted over to the woman he had indicated. A larger woman in her mid-forties, wearing a black coat and a polka dot hat.

"Hi, I'm Dory Sparks. I have been told you know Mr. Dellow."

"Well, I'm not sure I know him. Keeps himself to himself, that one."

"I am looking for him and haven't been able to get hold of him. He's not here, is he?"

"No, he never comes to the shelter."

"Have you seen him recently?"

"Now that you mention it, I think it's been a while. His house is fine, though. Walked past there earlier. I think I would have noticed if something had happened to it."

"Do you think there is a chance he has left London?"

"Can't see it. Has lived here every day of his life. Where would he go?"

"A relation, maybe."

"No. He was a foundling at the orphanage. Probably the by-blow of some tart. It was a rough neighborhood back then. No one cares about such things nowadays, but back then, there was quite a stigma attached to the foundlings. Conceived in sin, my old gran used to say. Nice enough man unless you get on the wrong side of him. Has a temper when he sees fit to."

"Anything he had a temper about lately?"

"Now I have heard, but I can't be sure about the truth, that he had some dispute with his neighbor some while back. And the publican at the Ruby Rose. Now he's a nasty fellow you don't want to cross. Wife left him. She used to turn up black and blue at times, makeup so heavy it caught flies. Good on her for taking off, I say. Now he's married to some young thing and will do the same to her."

"And Mr. Dellow had issue with him?"

"Love, I think Mr. Dellow was the type to have issue with most people. At heart, though, a decent man."

"Thank you. You have been wonderfully helpful."

The woman smiled with pride at the compliment, and Dory tried to make her cramped position more comfortable.

"Apparently bunk beds are being built for us, but they haven't turned up yet," the woman said. "The authorities never do anything around here unless you push 'em."

Chapter 29

THERE WERE QUITE a few new things that Dory had to record in her notebook, and a real suspect too—this publican at the Ruby Rose, which seemed a bit of a bruiser according to the telling. It was a clear lead and she would have to look into him. For a moment, she wondered if he was there in the shelter somewhere.

Well, if Mr. Dellow didn't shelter at night, perhaps this was the one time she would catch him at home. It wouldn't take long to rush over there and see if he was home. If not, then she could perhaps confirm that this man was missing. It would be enough to go to the police with.

Rising from her seat, Dory moved toward the exit.

"Where do you think you're going?" a warden said. "There's bombs falling out there."

Dory brought out her ATS identification. "There's always bombs falling out there. I'm afraid I must attend to something."

Grudgingly the man looked at her before he opened the door, as though she couldn't be trusted to make decisions for herself. Granted, she was putting herself at risk, but it wasn't this man's prerogative to say she couldn't.

A bomb fell nearby as soon as the door was closed behind her. Down from the stairwell, she could see the sparks of the shrapnel, even if the force of the explosion was absorbed by the sandbags. Bloody Germans.

Dory set off at a run toward Mr. Dellow's house. The streets were deserted and in the distance was the glow of fire, silhouetting the skyline. A truck rumbled down one of the side streets.

Unlike a blackout house where windows were covered, Mr. Dellow's house was just dark. No one came when she knocked and the door was firmly locked. It was dark next door as well, the neighbor she had initially spoken to, but she couldn't remember exactly what they'd said—if they had simply confirmed that he lived there or had said he was still around. Her poor record keeping was causing her problems yet again.

His house was at the end of a row, so most likely, it was this neighbor he had quarreled with, although that couldn't be taken for granted.

Walking around the outside of the house, she made her way into his backyard. Into a cobblestone area that had an old washing room and the outhouse. No one answered when she knocked there either, and for a moment, she wondered if she should break in. That would be highly illegal. There were patrols looking for looters and they probably wouldn't listen to her excuse.

Ridley would break in if he had reasonable suspicion that something untoward had happened to this man. Dory, however, didn't have that right. It was outside of her mandate to break into the house, even if she was so very curious as to what she would find out.

Looking around, she pulled out her flashlight and shone it into the house. Nothing was out of place in there. Her light swung over a plate of food and she swung back. It was half eaten and looked old. The potatoes had shrunken in on themselves.

Maybe she didn't need to break in. Dellow's deserted meal was evidence that he hadn't been there for a while.

Nothing else was out of place. He was a neat man, so it was unlikely he would simply forget to clear a plate of food for days on end. This was the first tangible proof that he really was missing, and she hadn't broken into his house to discover it.

Stepping back, she bumped into something and almost fell over. It was a washing basin, but there was darkness inside. Dory shone her light on it. Something was burnt. Leaning closer, she looked at it. It was just soot and char, but there were a few pieces of unburnt material and it looked like a rag rug, the multi-colored kind people made from old rags.

Who would burn a rug and why? And in a washing basin. The answer just appeared in her mind. It had been what he'd been carried in to Pennyfield Street, and then it had been burnt, because with his head wound, it had to have blood on it. The murderer had burnt it here after disposing of the body.

"Turn out that light, Frank!" a man said sharply from the other side of the brick wall. It was six feet tall, so she couldn't see him, but the flashlight must have reflected off the building. "Or I'll give you a fine." It had to be the warden responsible for this area. They were usually very happy to hand out fines for breaking the blackout.

"Not Frank," Dory replied.

"I don't care who you are. Turn it out all the same."

"It doesn't matter how black we are, the Germans still seem to find us with remarkable precision," Dory said tartly.

"We're to have complete blackout," the man stated.

"Fine, fine," Dory said and turned the light out.

"What you doing skulking around Frank's anyway?"

"I'm looking for him. I think something has happened to him."

"What do you mean something has happened to him?"

She could hear him coming around to the gate at the back and Dory shone her light at him. An older man with gray hair. "Put that down. And who are you?"

"Dory Sparks. ATS. No one has seen Frank Dellow, and his half-eaten food is decaying on his table. There's this burnt rug in here that I think was used to dispose of him."

"What are you talking about, girl?" the man said, his warden sleeve around his arm.

"I've been coming here for days. He's not answering. No one has seen him, and I think his body was found over on Pennyfield Street."

"That's miles away."

The man passed her and went to knock on the door. "Frank!" he yelled, but as before, nothing happened. "Hold this," he said handing over his bag, and went to break in the door with his shoulder, doing what Dory had been too squeamish to do, fearing she would get into trouble. This man obviously had no such fear.

It took a few tries, but the door gave suddenly. The air was stale inside. "Frank," the warden kept yelling.

This was the murder scene—Dory just knew it. He'd been having his supper and he'd been called away, probably by someone at the front door—someone he'd let in.

The warden walked up the narrow stairs to the second floor, and Dory followed as the man walked to the front room. A cage of steel and wood surrounded the bed, which was where Mr. Dellow slept at night. Dory had heard that people built such cages, but she wasn't sure if it would save someone if the house came down. It certainly wouldn't save anyone from the blast of a bomb. Some, though, preferred their beds at all costs.

The drone of planes passed over them and Dory held her breath, hoping nothing fell directly on her. The warden was staring up at the ceiling as if he could see through it. "He's not here," the warden said. "And you think he was found somewhere over on Pennyfield Street?"

"Yes," Dory said, walking downstairs again. In her gut, she knew that whatever guest he had let into his house, he wouldn't have taken them upstairs. As she shone her light around, she couldn't see anything suspicious. The lock to the door was intact. "I'll go to the police in the morning," she said as he walked into the front room, where a sofa and two chairs stood around a low table. A small piano sat along the wall and Dory was drawn to the pictures.

There was one in front of a church. It was old. Obviously his wedding picture. Leaning close to it, she stared. It was difficult to make out. Young men sometimes looked so different from their older selves. "This him?" she asked and the warden walked over. "Yep. Him and Martha. She passed some time ago."

The warden scratched his head, seemingly unsure what to do. "Poor Frank."

Obviously this man knew him well if he referred to him by his Christian name. "He had some quarrels with people," she said.

"What's that got to do with bombs dropping on his head?"

"I don't think it was a bomb that killed him. I think someone did—someone he invited in."

"Or perhaps you're just being fanciful," the man said.

"Maybe," Dory said without offense. "It was just that he was found in the rubble of a collapsed building without any dust on him. How many bodies do you know that come out clean from a building collapse?" As a warden, he saw quite a few of them. And what she said made perfect sense to him.

"Bastards," he finally said.

"I think he was killed here and carried over to Pennyfield Street in that burnt rug out back. About three weeks ago."

"Maybe I can identify him."

"He's already been buried, but they'd have a picture of him at the morgue at Great London Hospital. It would confirm it if you can identify him. I didn't know him and I can't tell from this photo," she said, holding up the gilt frame with Frank Dellow's wedding photo. "Sorry, what was your name?"

"David Wilkens."

"I'll go over and have a look in the morning," he said, sounding defeated. "Poor Frank. Who'd do this?"

"I don't know yet. But I'm going to find out."

Chapter 30

MR. DELLOW'S STREET was not in the Limehouse police's jurisdiction, so she had to go the Poplar police station, where she'd never been before. A yellow brick building with bars on all the windows. It was certainly not inviting, but she walked in to approach the desk.

"I need to speak to a detective about a body found on Pennyfield Street."

"Oh, aye," the desk sergeant said without any infliction or surprise. "The body is there now?"

"No, the body was removed some three weeks ago."

"Well, we're a bit short on DIs at the moment. You will have to speak to Sunderson." The desk sergeant picked up the phone and spoke to someone. "Go through, he'll meet you there," the man said, indicating to a door.

Dory did so, feeling a little like she was walking into the unknown, but a young man stood there, dressed in his blue uniform. "Sorry, what was your name?"

"Dory Sparks," she said. "Are you Sunderson?" The man couldn't be older than her; she had been expecting someone more experienced.

"Now, tell me about this body."

Dory went on to explain everything, including the circumstances of the body and the absence of Mr. Dellow from his house. Also the disagreements mentioned with neighbors and the publican of the Ruby Rose. The groan from his lips suggested he knew the public well.

The young man took notes and then put them to side. "I'll look into it. Please leave your contact details with the desk, in case we need to be in touch with you."

She was dismissed, and Dory took a few seconds to realize it. "Right," she said. "There's nothing I can do to help?"

"You've been very helpful in bringing this matter to us."

"No offense, Mr. Sunderland, but I had expected a detective to take a case like this, considering it is likely murder."

"Well, we are running short on those. The military keep pinching them," a slight note of exasperation in his voice.

"I am aware," Dory said with a smile. "Intelligence, I believe."

"Rightly so," he said with surprise, regarding her anew. "I'll let you know what we find. We'll definitely question Jimmy Magren. Bad lot, that one."

"So I've heard." She assumed that was the publican.

There was nothing further to say, and Dory searched her mind in case there was something she'd forgotten. She could always come back, she justified as she walked through the back of the police station, where a number of desks stood stacked in a large room, files stacked neatly on top of others.

It was a good feeling walking out of the police station. They hadn't dismissed her claim and would look into it. Mr. Dellow might get some justice for his life being cut short. The question of why still clawed at her. Why would someone do this? What could possibly be so worthy that it justified taking someone's life? She couldn't understand.

Returning home, Vera was in the kitchen with the paper spread out across the table. Her lips were nicely rouged from the beetroot lipstick. Not a full red, more like a mix between red and pink. It suited her coloring.

"Anything interesting?" Dory asked.

"Same old guff. Oh, a letter came for you."

"Right," Dory said and walked over to the small table in the hall were they sometimes left letters. It was a blue envelope, unlike any she had seen before. This wasn't the nice, creamy blue paper Lady Pettifer used, or the thin tissue-like paper her mother used. Ripping it open, Dory pulled out the letter. A neat, curving hand, suggesting that Mr. Jones would like to personally thank her and to call on him at her earliest opportunity.

Dory's eyebrows rose in surprise. Perhaps it wasn't a surprise. If she had been in his position, she would feel moved to thank the person who had rescued her. It wasn't necessary. Finding his situation had been a by-product of her investigation into Mr. Dellow's death. Discovering the injustice done to Mr. Jones had simply been fortuitous. But she would go meet him, understanding that it was important to him to thank his rescuer.

Returning to the kitchen, Dory cut herself two slices of bread and a piece of cheese.

"The cabbages we planted aren't coming up at all," Vera said. "I don't hold out much hope for the carrots either. We haven't got a green thumb between us."

"That's a shame."

"Apparently it's going to be another couple of days before the searchlight is operational. There was some shrapnel damage and the mirror inside shattered. Another one is being sent from Manchester, but it will take a few days. To tell you the truth, I'm getting sick of dancing every night."

"Never thought I'd see that day," Dory said.

"Besides, looks like it will be a clear night tonight."

A respite would do them all some good.

"I like your lipstick."

"Do you want some? I made heaps of it."

"Sure," Dory said. It was a shame she didn't have it when Ridley had visited. She would definitely keep some for when he came again. A thrill of nervousness shot down her body thinking they would have another day together.

Vera went upstairs to her room and returned with a small pot. "Don't go wild, because we probably won't get any more glycerin for a while."

"Thank you," Dory said. She would put some on before she left. Might as well go see Mr. Jones in the afternoon, get it over with while she had this time off work.

*

The façade of Mr. Jones building looked exactly the same as before. Everything down this street looked so calm, it was hard to think that a vicious crime was being committed behind one of these doors. Walking up the stairs to number sixteen, Dory knocked.

A young man answered the door, one Dory hadn't met before. "I'm here to see Mr. Jones," she said. "Miss Dory Sparks."

"Ah, yes. He is in his study. This way," the man said, leading her over to the right side of the house, toward a set of double doors, which slid apart to a warm space with a dark desk and matching chairs. Mr. Jones sat in a chair by the fire, a blanket over his legs. He looked different from the terrified and scraggly man who she'd seen lying in bed.

Like this, he seemed much more like the solicitor he was—formidable even as he still looked ill. The corner of his lip drooped slightly.

"Miss Sparks," he said and Dory tentatively sat down in the opposite chair. The heat of the fire stung her cold hands from the brisk weather outside. "It's a pleasure to see you. I was hoping you'd come. Some tea?" His speech had a slight slur to it from his stroke, but he looked a hundred times better than he had.

"Tea would be lovely. I'm glad to see you're feeling better."

"Yes. Harper will organize some tea," he said to the young man who was still standing at the door. "He is a reliable man after those harpies," he said. "Both been charged and I believe both will face jail for what they did. I wish to thank you, of course. It was your persistence that got me the help I needed." His voice was labored and it was difficult for him to talk.

"Well, I am glad their deeds were uncovered."

"Harpies," the man repeated with distaste. "Well, I am in your debt if you shall ever need it. Is there anything you need?"

"Not really," she said. "I am just glad you are better, and recovering from… your ordeal."

"Then it will be a standing debt."

The young man brought a silver tea service and gently placed it down on the table, before pouring two delicate teacups. Dory accepted hers. It was good tea and she savored it. Would it be uncouth to ask for some tea to take away, Dory wondered with a smile. She wouldn't take the man's tea from him. Enough had been taken from him as it was.

"So I have been told you are a member of the ATS."

"That is right. I man one of the searchlights down toward the docks."

"Perilous work," he said. "The police also told me that you were on the hunt for the identity of a man found after one of the raids. You have asserted through unnatural causes. You found me as part of that quest."

"Yes," Dory agreed.

"Any success?"

"I believe I have found his identity. The police are now looking into it, so I don't know who or why just yet, but hopefully we'll know soon."

"The man deserves his justice. I count myself lucky to be discovered in the process. I live to tell the tale. This war seems to drive some to wicked deeds indeed." For a moment he was lost in thoughts. "But there have always been those who seek opportunity for wickedness. The disorder simply gives them a greater chance to." He spoke with an assurance from years of practicing law. In that capacity, he must have seen the very worst of human nature.

Chapter 31

DORY'S CURIOSITY REFUSED to let her stay away, and on the way home, she walked past Mr. Dellow's house. The front door was open and there was still a policeman inside, taking photos. The flash flared through the windows, and there was a crowd of people outside. The police were certainly taking this seriously.

Among the crowd, she spotted the warden she'd been dealing with last night. It seemed an age ago, but it had only been last night. Everything was moving so fast now. It was as if a dam had burst and everything flooded out.

When the warden spotted her, he moved toward her. "Miss Sparks," he said.

"Mr. Wilkens. Did you get a chance to go to the hospital?"

"That I did, and after some fluffing around, they showed me a picture of Frank. It is him that was found on Pennyfield Street."

In a way, it was all more sad now that they had an identity for the man. He became more of a person instead of simply a body.

"The police are treating it as a homicide," he said. "I understand they hauled in Jimmy Magren this afternoon. He's still there, but his wife says he's not responsible. Says he's never been missing during the raids. Obviously the police won't put much stock on her words, but there's a shelter full of people and only one of them need to recall his presence."

"Could it be that he didn't do it?" Dory asked.

Mr. Wilkens shrugged. "It wouldn't surprise me if he did. Who else would have done it? The man is certainly fond of using his fists."

"Yet scared of the Germans," Dory said.

"There was definitely a raid that night?" he asked.

"Yes, I even saw the bomb drop on Pennyfield Street."

"Well, it isn't impossible to sneak out of a shelter in the wee hours when everyone is sleeping. People get up to relieve themselves all night, so no one would bat an eyelid at someone walking around. He could well have snuck off and done the deed."

"We know Mr. Dellow was killed early evening while he ate his supper," Dory said.

"Could be that he lay around dead for hours before Magren came and carted him away. He is certainly strong enough to carry a body."

Dory hadn't seen this Jimmy Magren, but she took his word for it.

As they watched, Sunderson in his uniform and with his hat under his arm, stepped out of the neighbor's house, putting away the notebook he'd been writing in. He'd been questioning the neighbor, and seemed pleased with the result. The woman with a lined face and sharp features followed, wearing a flower print apron and a shawl over her hair. She crossed her arms and regarded the scene, standing on her doorstep. Her taller daughter appeared behind her, also curious about the commotion outside. She had rouged cheeks and red lips. Pretty in a fleeting way.

"What was the nature of the quarrel between Mr. Dellow and his neighbor?" she asked Mr. Wilkens.

"I don't know the details. Mr. Dellow could be a cantankerous man when it came to some. He didn't suffer fools gladly." His tone suggested that he hadn't much respect for the neighbor either.

"Mother and daughter, isn't it?" Dory said.

"That's right. Crewes is the name. Used to be married to Harry Crewes, but he died some time ago. Dock worker. Well, I think the fun's over," Wilkens said. "It's getting dark."

"The Germans won't come for a while yet," Dory said. "They'll come with that front over there," she said, pointing to clouds sitting to the east "And it's slow moving. I'd say the sirens won't sound until midnight, if at all."

"Have learned to read the clouds, have you?"

"I've been standing around watching every night. They won't come while it's too clear. Too easy to see in the moonlight. Moon's close to full."

"You might be wasted on the searchlights, Miss Sparks," he said with a snort before moving away.

Dory stayed to watch. The police were winding down their examination and people were losing interest. Perhaps like Mr. Wilkens, fearing the night too much to stick around.

Constable Sunderland was heading toward a car and Dory ran to intercept him. "Miss Sparks. I'm surprised to see you here."

"Are you?" Dory didn't see why. "I was walking past. I understand Mr. Wilkens has confirmed the identity of the body at the hospital through photographs."

"So I understand. The hospital called me." He looked impatient.

"He also said you've been questioning Jimmy Magren."

"Your Mr. Wilken is very informed, isn't he?"

"Everyone knows everyone's business around here. Did he do it?"

"We're still trying to break his alibi, but the neighbor here has just confirmed seeing him earlier in the night, so I think there is a good chance he'll be charged. Obviously, I expect you will keep this information to yourself."

"Of course," she said. "And motive?"

"Well, Magren is a violent man. There was a confrontation at the pub some weeks back. Dellow accused him of watering down the drinks. Magren ordered Dellow out of his establishment. The details are still sketchy."

That was hardly motive, Dory thought. That bothered her. It didn't make sense if there wasn't a motive. Maybe it was a motive to some. Wasn't every single publican in the city accused of watering down drinks?

"We found some blood splatter inside. Faint, but definitely there," Sunderson continued. "The man was murdered alright."

Dory shuddered at the thought. "Do you know the nature of his disagreements with the neighbor?"

"Noise and something to do with whiffy garbage," he said. "Normal things neighbors get pissy at each other about."

Didn't really sound like motive either unless dealing with someone clearly unhinged. "As you are done here, would you mind if I have a look inside?"

"I thought you'd already been inside."

"It was dark. I'd like to see if there is anyone he corresponded with that should be contacted."

Sunderson breathed deeply as if he really wanted to say no. "Fine, but I want you to lock the door. If I hear of you stealing anything, I'll have you nicked."

"I'm not going to steal anything," Dory said, finally offended.

"Just giving you a warning. The sirens will go off in a minute."

Dory grumbled her goodbye and stepped inside the house. The crowd outside had dispersed and Dory turned the light on. The blood splatter was still difficult for her to see, but she took their word for it. Mr. Dellow had clearly invited his murderer into the house and they had proceeded to whack him on the back of the head judging by the injuries, likely when his back was turned. The invited person was apparently trusted enough that Mr. Dellow would turn his back on them. That would hardly be Mr. Magren, would it?

Things felt wrong, but she couldn't exactly say what. Probably because the motive didn't make sense. With all the murders she had seen—both of the murders she had seen—the motive was blatantly clear. The murderer saw the act as necessary, but simply bashing someone over the head because of watered down drinks—that seemed mad.

It had to be something else entirely. Perhaps Dory would speak to the man's wife. The police were always dismissive of wives, believing their testimony to be inherently suspicious, but Dory didn't hold those same beliefs. Next chance she got, she would head over to the Ruby Rose to speak to Mrs. Magren.

The house was utterly silent and Dory walked into the living room. Everything was dusted. Mr. Dellow was a house-proud man, who took care of his property and things. All the furniture was old and worn. Maybe they had been new at one time, likely at the start of his marriage, but had worn down over time.

Walking over to the desk, Dory sat down and looked through. It seemed wrong that there was no one to inform. There had to be people who cared for him and should know of his death even if he didn't have any direct family as such.

There was stationary, and a few letters from a vicar somewhere in Devon. The letters were familiar in tone, so they had to be friends. Maybe even all the way back to the orphanage. Dory took the envelope with the return address, determining that she would write to this man.

A bill from a coal merchant caught her eye, but there was nothing remarkable about it. Simply delivery of a set amount of coal. There was also a torn newspaper advert about the destruction of a part of the docks.

It reminded her that she should check if he'd been cashing his pension checks regularly or if someone else had been doing it for him. Pensions were coveted, it seemed.

Lastly in the pile, which looked like new correspondence, there was a letter from the council saying the files he had ordered were ready for review. It said nothing else and Dory put it to side. Nothing seemed totally out of the ordinary, but she put an envelope from the vicar in her bag. Perhaps Mr. Dellow had confided in him and knew of some threat to his person. Maybe he also knew of some deeper running dispute between Dellow and Magren beyond the quality of drinks.

Chapter 32

A LETTER ARRIVED the next day from Lady Pettifer containing a train ticket for Christmas Eve.

You must come visit us, it had said. With all the sadness and distress, celebrating Christmas is more important than ever.

Dory sighed as she read it. It was hard to get Lady Pettifer to understand that the Germans set the schedule. They couldn't simply get up and leave because they wanted to be somewhere else. These things made no sense to Lady Pettifer who would probably call Churchill himself to berate him for forcing the ATS girls to work over Christmas.

But really, if she had the day off, she really should be spending it with her mother in Swanley. Dory could well imagine that Lady Pettifer would solve that problem by saying she could simply drive down to Swanley for Christmas Day. Everything was simple and solvable to Lady Pettifer.

If only she could stop the Luftwaffe from coming.

Of course Lady Pettifer had anticipated her objections, which was why she sent a train ticket that had already been paid for.

Maybe the Germans would want to celebrate Christmas too, and they would all have some time off, but then there had been a severely anti-religious stance to the Nazis, which could mean that they rejected Christmas as well. Who knew? Nothing the Germans did was logical to Dory.

Setting off from home, Dory bought herself a cup of soup from the mobile canteen. In all their time off, no one in the house had thought to go to the shop. They had run out of practically everything. None of the three of them could be accused of being domestic successes, especially perhaps as they had simply grown to accept that the wall to their kitchen was mostly gone.

Dory had to put the musings of her domestic failings aside as she walked toward the Ruby Rose. It was probably not open yet, but Dory could knock. The Magrens would live on the upper story.

Doing just that. Dory waited. Maybe she couldn't be heard, so she banged harder.

"We're not open," a woman finally said from the window above. She had curlers in her hair as she glared down at Dory.

"I need to speak to you about your husband."

"What about my husband?" she said in a sharp voice.

"Could we speak inside?"

"No."

"Alright. Do you think he killed Mr. Dellow?" Dory yelled, a little bit as punishment for making her have this conversation out in the street in full view of the entire street.

"You from the paper?"

"No, I am the one who found Mr. Dellow." Technically that was true. "I am trying to find out who killed him."

"I'll be right down," the woman finally said and disappeared. When she came to the door, she was surprisingly short. "Come in," she said and eyed the street suspiciously. A pub looked oddly bare without any people. "My Jimmy's never killed anyone, and I won't hear of anyone saying anything else."

"Well, the police seem to think so," Dory said.

"They're trying to pin this on Jimmy and it's unfair."

"They say Mr. Magren and Mr. Dellow quarreled."

"Jimmy quarrels with anyone who gives him lip in his establishment. It's his right."

"There was nothing else?"

"Why would there be? Frank Dellow was just some old codger. Whined about everyone and everything. If anyone murdered him it'd be the people that were forced to listen to him. Jimmy kicked him out for being lippy. That's all. Besides, he spends hardly anything, sits around for hours nursing a measly pint. We can't have the place filled up with those. We'd never make ends meet. If someone killed him, it weren't my Jimmy."

"Mr. Dellow was a dock worker before he retired, I think."

"So?"

"Well, they all stick together, don't they?" Dory had no idea where she was going with this. Perhaps Frank had threatened Jimmy in some way that would affect his business.

"No, they don't. Not when a pint's involved. And not for the likes of Frank Dellow. Not exactly Mr. Popularity."

"Who else didn't like him?"

The girl's face clouded over a little. "It's not so much that they hate him. He's just hard work, isn't he? Always got his back up about something. You'd say it was cold outside and he'd argue with you even if it was snowing. Argued about absolutely everything. But no one took him seriously. He was just like that. Cantankerous. Some go like that when they age, don't they? Maybe he was always like that. His wife must have been a saint."

The girl was either a very accomplished liar, or she was telling the truth. She had a naturalness about her that was hard to replicate. It was a shame she had aligned herself with someone like Jimmy Magren, if the rumors about him were true. But then she certainly wasn't some mouse scurrying around in the shadows. This girl seemed to have her own opinions.

"You go to the shelter down the road at night, don't you?" Dory asked.

"Every night. And I would have noticed if Jimmy fucked off and carted some body around half the night. I'm not an idiot. He didn't go out that night or any other night. I swear it."

Perhaps it was Dory's trusting nature, but she wanted to believe her. It was hard for her to doubt something someone was earnestly saying to her. Anyway, there was no trace of some underlying alibi coming from this corner—unless Jimmy Magren found Mr. Dellow annoying to the point of murdering him. There had to be something else—but what? And where could she turn to ask?

That woman, Mrs. Simpson, would have said if there was anything deeper, but she would perhaps know someone who knew this couple better than she did. It might be an avenue worth exploring.

Saying goodbye, Dory took her leave and didn't quite know what to do with herself. She had no idea where Mrs. Simpson lived, but she had to be nearby. There wouldn't be time to go to the shelter tonight, because the searchlight would be fixed and it would be back to normal come nightfall.

Dory had to take to asking random people on the street, but she was finally pointed in a direction and was led to a green door in a set of terrace houses.

"Yes?" the woman said when she opened the door.

"Mrs. Simpson. I am Dory Sparks. We spoke the other day."

"So we did. I see you survived the night fleeing into the dropping bombs. I also understand that the police have been looking for poor Frank Dellow's murderer. Frightful, isn't it?"

"They are questioning Jimmy Magren."

"I'm not surprised."

"Still, though, haven't really caught wind on a motive. For murder, I find stronger motive than a simple quarrel is usually the case. The only thing that ties him is a sighting by the neighbor, Mrs. Crewes." Only after did Dory realize she had just let slip something she had promised to keep secret, and she had done it to the biggest gossip around. How could she have been so stupid? Dory was mortified by her own carelessness. Could she have just jeopardized the whole investigation with her loose lips. She hadn't even thought.

"I'd heard," Mrs. Simpson said and Dory visibly relaxed. It was common knowledge. Perhaps the police were not so good at keeping their own secrets, or maybe Mrs. Crewes was spreading this knowledge far and wide.

"Do you think she is credible?"

Mrs. Simpson looked surprised by the question. "I don't see why she would lie. In a court of law, she might be challenged, though. Been known to cheat when she can. Had some stolen ration book she tried to present. Got told off for it. Everyone knows. Her husband was a little the same. You wouldn't feel comfortable having him in your house in case something disappeared. Sly and cunning the lot of them. Still, I can't see her lying about something so serious. I wouldn't say she is a downright malicious type. Just don't trust her with your wallet if you know what's good for you."

"She didn't have anything against Mr. Magren, did she?"

"No. There were some run-ins between the late Mr. Crewes and Jimmy, but everyone had run-ins with Jimmy. If Mrs. Crewes says she saw him, then she probably did. Never been a fault with her eyes."

Dory leaned back in her seat. This still wasn't giving her anything. If Mrs. Crewes saw him around the time Dellow was murdered, that did suggest he'd done it, but there was still nothing like a proper motive.

"Do you know anyone who would know of a deeper reason why Jimmy Magren would murder Mr. Dellow, some reason other than complaining about the service at the Ruby Rose?"

Putting her fingers to her lips, Mrs. Simpson thought for a while. "I suppose you could go speak to his ex-wife. If anyone would know, it would be her, but she left London some while ago."

"Do you know where she is?"

"Can't say that I do."

Well, that didn't help, Dory thought.

"I'll make some tea and you can tell me about how you discovered Mr. Dellow's murder. I hear it makes an interesting tale."

Was there anything this woman didn't hear about?

Chapter 33

THE GERMANS CAME that night and Dory lost herself finding them in the dark skies above. The searchlight was functional, but it had a kink whenever she moved it to the left. It worked, though, and that was the important part. Vera searched the skies as she normally did, giving direction when she could.

Dory had almost forgotten the heat of the lamp, which was more pleasant in the cold. Light drizzle steamed off the searchlight drum.

Lady Pettifer's train ticket returned to her mind and the sea of indecisiveness that came with it. Technically, she could go at dawn and return on the 3 o'clock train. Then repeat the same thing to Swanley the next day. It would mean a remarkable lack of sleep, but everyone would be happy.

Dory knew Lady Pettifer hadn't invited her to cause trouble, but she really wanted to see her, and in some way insisting the ATS weren't abusing her. Visitors would also be a reprieve from the constant worry over Andrew, her son, and Vivian. Maybe even Cedric. Although safe in America, he certainly wouldn't be safe if he was crossing the Atlantic. The *Athenia* and the *City of Bendares*, both sailing to Canada with a load full of evacuee children could attest to that. The oceans were not safe for anyone. No one was safe anywhere, it seemed.

Then there was the next step in her investigation to continue. In the morning, she would write to Mr. Dellow's vicar friend, and hopefully the man would write back. Who knew what would come of that?

And lastly, the former Mrs. Magren, who no one seemed to know the whereabouts of these days. But there had been a divorce, so there must be a solicitor and even a barrister dealing with it. They would perhaps know in which part of the country she now resided. The courthouse would have the records. Perhaps she could ask Mr. Jones to advise her if it proved difficult. It shouldn't, though. Court records were public.

Compared to other nights, the Germans seemed a bit half-hearted. It wasn't a heavy night of bombardment, nor were there endless waves of planes. They came, dropping their load and were off again. Hopefully not too much damage would be inflicted. Perhaps they near froze to death up there and were all keen to get back to their bases. Bitterly, Dory hoped so. She hoped they suffered physically and also with their conscience for what they did night after night.

At around three in the morning, the bombing appeared to stop. They waited and searched, but they heard no more planes coming.

"Guess they're cutting out early tonight," Vera said, dragging her seat closer to the searchlight. "When are they ever going to stop? It's not like they're achieving anything. By now we're so used to it, it's almost second nature."

That was far from true, but Dory understood Vera's point. "If we haven't broken by now, we're hardly going to." Still, though, people were tired of having to huddle underground every night, emerging to possible homelessness. Tempers were fraying and the cold wasn't helping as few had enough coal to keep warm.

Were they actually winning this war? Were they achieving anything? Or was this all going to end with the Germans knocking on doors down in Dover?

A shiver ran up Dory's spine at the thought. The idea of Germans marching into London was terrifying. What would be the best thing to do in that case? Escape? To where? She would always be welcome at Wallisford Hall, but that might be the worst place to be. In Poland, the Germans had been brutal to the landowning class. There was nothing to say they wouldn't be here too.

Dory could well remember how some of the gentlemen and ladies of higher standing had quite admired Mr. Hitler before the war. Surely they didn't do so now. It went to show how very wrong they could be in their assessment. A fine education didn't necessarily make people intelligent.

It was a dull few hours until dawn, but it finally crested and Dory turned off her searchlight. With having the days off, her sleep patterns were out of whack. Perhaps she would have a proper sleep before she sought out the nearest courthouse. Betsy would know where to find it. Apparently her father had appeared before the judge a time or two.

They all walked home together as the people of the city emerged from their hiding places and started their days.

They walked past a woman whose skirt was beyond a doubt made from curtains. Even the sun fade was visible in waves across the material. But at least she had a new skirt. Perversely, it made Dory wonder what would happen to Mr. Dellow's clothes. And his house. With the number of homeless, surely they wouldn't leave it sitting empty. Without an heir, his estate would be given over to the crown, unless some distant next of kin could be found. Would they even know of this man? It was common in old novels that people received a surprise inheritance from some relative that they'd never known about.

They all went to sleep shortly after arriving at home, to wake shortly after one in the afternoon. The drizzle still fell outside the window and it was a gray, dull day. Dory pulled on a fresh shirt before dressing in her uniform again. She was sick to death of the dull green she had to wear every day. If she had some nice curtains, she would have designs on them as well. With longing, she remembered the beautiful, summery dresses she had worn in France. It seemed a lifetime ago.

"I'm heading out," she called into the kitchen, going straight for the door, heading for the telephone box down the road. The telephone book hung on a chain. There weren't that many courts in London, the most likely for a divorcing couple from here had to be the Tower Bridge Magistrates Court. More money had to be spent on bus fares. It wasn't cheap this sleuthing business, but hopefully her next step would be revealed either by the vicar or the former Mrs. Magren. Those were the two avenues of inquiries she had before her.

The building she sought was stone and brick, and imposing in the way Victorian buildings were. It wasn't a place of levity and Dory felt the somber atmosphere as soon as she walked in. People spoke in hushed voices and dressed in old-fashioned wig and gowns. The office of the court clerks was located on the second floor and Dory walked up a gray stone staircase.

There was a queue and she stood patiently until it was her turn to speak to the bespectacled thin man behind the desk. Here was someone who could benefit from a bit of sun, Dory thought as she contemplated how to go about this. If there was a special language she was supposed to use. In lieu of, she simply stated what she wanted. Maybe she did need Mr. Jones' assistance after all. "I wish to gain access to the records for the divorce of a Mr. Jimmy Magren."

"Date?" the man said with absolutely no enthusiasm and pulled over a piece of paper to write on.

"I don't know. He is the publican in the Ruby Rose."

The man looked unimpressed. "Return in two weeks. I'll see if I can find it." With that, she was dismissed. Two weeks. That was an eternity away, but what choice did she have? It wasn't as if she could go back there and search herself, like she had at the hospital. Even the ATS could not get into the court archives.

So she went outside. There was nothing for her to do but wait. Although it was nice to sit down by the river. The last time she had done so had been with Captain Ridley.

In her mind, she could imagine herself writing to him, reporting that she had solved the murder of Mr. Dellow. Hopefully he would be impressed. She would be impressed with herself if she solved it. It was by far more difficult to solve than the other two she had been involved with. This one felt more like pulling teeth, and she'd have no idea what to do next if nothing came of speaking to either the vicar or the former Mrs. Magren.

Two weeks. How did anyone in the city get anything done if they had to wait two weeks? It seemed to be common, though, if one wanted information from the official services or municipalities. A memory of the letter in Mr. Dellow's desk returned to her mind. He'd done the same thing. Had requested information from the council. She wondered what for. What had he been searching for?

Thinking of it now, it seemed an important question. What *had* he been searching for? It was obviously something he'd been willing to wait weeks to collect. Had he collected it? She didn't know. If nothing else in these two weeks of waiting, she could find out what he'd requested and if he'd collected it. There was nothing in his house that had looked like records of any kind. And if he had collected it, what had he done with it?

Chapter 34

IT WAS A RUSH TO GET to the city council building before it closed, and longer to stand in the queue. It seemed she did endless amounts of standing in queues of late. How much of her free time was spent standing in queues? It was part of the price of getting something.

The clerk looked tired by the time she got to the front of the line.

"I'm here about some files ordered by Mr. Frank Dellow," she said to the woman.

"You hardly look like a Frank."

"No, Mr. Dellow is incapacitated," she said, not finding an appropriate way to say that he'd been topped off and whatever was in those files might tell her why. It was simply easier to imply he was unable to get the files, which was technically true.

"One moment," the woman said, then walked over to a filing cabinet and sliding the top shelf open. Finally, she lifted out a manila envelope. "You can't take these away. You can view them, then you give them back to me."

"Of course," Dory said, accepting the envelope almost fearing that the woman would change her mind. Curiosity coursed through her as she carried the envelope away to a tall table over to the side. The envelope had been used again and again, with names scratched out. The one that wasn't said 'Frank Dellow.'

Unwinding the tie, Dory opened the flap and pulled out the documents inside. There were three separate bundles. The letterhead was from the Ministry of Works, and this was about some kind of application for compensation regarding building damage.

Dory started from the beginning and read, but it was as though she only got part of the story, because this was a response to some application. The application wasn't actually in here. It referred to a sum of one hundred and twenty pounds, which was a fair bit of money. For war-related damage to number forty-one Hurst Street.

Well, that was Mr. Dellow's street, but there wasn't any damage to his house—unless he'd had it fixed. It could be windows and he had the means of getting new window glass, she supposed. That wouldn't cost anywhere near one hundred and twenty pounds, though. She checked the date and this was from three months ago.

Dory couldn't make heads or tails of this. There were no repairs to Mr. Dellow's house. It would be visible.

Putting it to the side, she checked the second bundle, which was a second response, this time for the sum of one hundred pounds, dated two months ago. Checking the third, it was the same for ninety pounds one month and a half ago.

Were these three separate applications for damage? Across all three, she checked the address. All for forty-one Hurst Street. Each had a stamp on them saying 'Dispursed.'

What in the world was going on? Why would there be three lots of compensation? Was that how compensation was distributed? Three lots over three months? But there was no damage.

Something wasn't right here. Dory read again. War-related damage the letters all said, which could only be for bomb damage, unless troops were moving through and caused damage, which didn't really happen so much in the East End. So this was for bomb damage, but there was no damage. Maybe the roof?

Bundling up the documents, Dory returned to the desk, getting a filthy look from the person next in line. "Excuse me. Does war-related compensation get doled out in three lots?"

"War-related damage?" the woman said. "No, lump sum."

Dory's eyebrows rose.

"Excuse me," the woman next in line said tartly and elbowed Dory out of the way. Dory was too caught up with the implications of this to care.

There were three claims for compensation. Even a roof would not get damaged three months in a row. The odds would be astronomical.

"We're closing soon. Are you ready to hand those back?"

"In a moment," Dory said, quickly returning to the examination table. Pulling out her notebook, she copied down the vital details of each claim and then returned the envelope.

Why would Mr. Dellow have retrieved these files? Was he trying to destroy the records? Hand them back with vital pieces of information missing?

As Dory wandered out of the building, she flipped through her notebook to her conversation with the librarian, who had said Mr. Dellow had complained about municipal organizations. Not about the actual council structure perhaps, more the management of municipal activities.

Flipping back to the latest entry, she reviewed the details and it struck her. Mr. Dellow wasn't at forty-one; he was at thirty-nine. This was about the neighbor. He was tracing her activities with claiming compensation for damage to her building—which didn't have any particular damage that she could see. Three applications for compensation in three months, or fairly substantial sums of money.

And they had argued. Dory bet it hadn't been about the noise as the woman had said. Frank had likely confronted her about her activities, and she'd killed him—then claimed she'd seen Jimmy Magren there early that evening. The neighbor was the only one linking Jimmy Magren to the murder, and it was a diversion.

Obviously, she wasn't strong enough to carry Mr. Dellow over to Pennyfield Street, although people, usually men, underestimated how strong women were, but between her and her daughter, who was a stout woman, they could have done it. Being retired, Mr. Dellow hadn't been the heartiest of men. They could have carried him off.

Mrs. Crewes had motive, and she had opportunity. By her own false admission in seeing Magren there, she implied that she was there too. Something blunt had been used to bash Mr. Dellow over the head.

Why hadn't she looked for a murder weapon when she'd been there? She hadn't even thought about it.

Finally, Dory noticed that the sun was setting. It was getting dark and the day was ending. She should be making her way over to the searchlight, but she wanted to inform Constable Sunderson of what she'd learnt before he went home for the evening. Poor Jimmy Magren—or perhaps poor was the wrong word for him, but he was innocent of murder— and was still languishing in jail at the station.

At a sprint, Dory headed over the police station, telling the desk sergeant that she had vital information that she needed to tell Constable Sunderson.

"He's out," the man said.

For some reason, Dory hadn't expected this. "Can he be reached?"

"Don't know exactly where he is, but he should be back in the next hour or so. You can come back then."

"I can't. I have to man the searchlight down by the docks."

"Then I can take a message," the man said, pulling over a piece of paper.

"Okay, right," Dory said, trying to get her mind sorted. "Tell him that I know who killed Mr. Dellow."

"Oh, aye," the sergeant said, suddenly more interested.

"It isn't Jimmy Magren," she continued, "instead, Mrs. Crewes and her daughter, or or one of them. To do with bomb damage claims. There is evidence of applications at the city council offices. I just came from there, a total sum of…" —she checked her notebook— "three hundred and ten pounds."

The sergeant had run out of paper and his writing was getting smaller and smaller. "I'll give this to him as soon as he arrives. And you are?"

"Dory Sparks. We've met. He has my details if he needs to be in touch. But tell him that the files will probably be sent back to the Ministry of Works tomorrow, so he needs to claim them first thing, or else try to request them again."

Quickly, she checked her watch. "I have to go. The bloody Germans will probably be early today." With the rain and cloud cover, they would have no reason to wait. Most likely they were already on their way. For all the purpose of keeping the weather outlook confidential, the Germans seemed to predict the weather just fine without their help.

As she ran down the street, a feeling of pride and completion filled her. She'd solved the case; she knew it in her bones. From nothing making sense, everything suddenly made sense. The neighbor had killed him, not for money, but still for greed, and for not being caught defrauding the Government.

As Mr. Jones would attest, the war was seen as an opportunity by some, and they took advantage using the most despicable means. Perhaps people who would never actually do such things under normal circumstances. This wasn't normal circumstances and some people's minds shifted because of this.

Dory couldn't wait to tell Lady Pettifer what she had learnt—and Ridley. She would write him tomorrow and tell him that she had solved this case. She'd never been so proud of anything in her life.

It was nearing dark and Dory ran up the stairs.

"About time you got here. You seem to be later and later every day," Vera chided her.

"Not anymore," Dory said with a smile. "I no longer have a reason to be late."

"Well, you can tell me why later. Right now, though, we got to get the light up and running. The observers have already picked them up down by the coast. They're on their way. Early tonight, aren't they?"

Chapter 35

BY THE LOOKS OF IT, it was going to be a heavy night of bombardment.

"Sending us a bloody Christmas present, aren't they, the bastards," Vera said at one point. "I wish we were better at shooting them down."

The Bofors gun across the river was firing nonstop, traces lit up across the sky.

"If they let us on the guns as opposed to those older gentlemen, we could probably do a better job," she continued. They weren't allowed to man the guns. Fighting was strictly seen as a man's job even when women had proved to be just as good as men at just about everything. Still weren't allowed on the guns.

A noise behind them caught Dory's attention and she turned to see Constable Sunderson in his dark blue uniform. "I understood I could find you here," he said.

"We're a bit busy," Vera stated, but Sunderson ignored her.

"Those lights are hot, aren't they?" he said as he moved closer. "I got a garbled message from the desk sergeant saying you know who killed Mr. Dellow."

"Yes, the neighbor, Mrs. Crewes, and her daughter. I don't know exactly which killed him, but they both had to carry him over to Pennyfield Street. They have been making false applications for compensation for damage to their house and Mr. Dellow was onto them. I think he confronted them, and they killed him."

"And what proof do you have of this?"

"Just the applications and the fact that Mr. Dellow had requested to see the files."

"That's not concrete proof."

Dory hadn't expected this reticence, but she finally understood. "It's more of a motive than Magren has." They wanted Magren to be guilty because he was an ongoing problem. Sadly, he just wasn't. "It's only Mrs. Crewes who places him at the scene and she did so to divert from herself."

"Didn't mean he wasn't there."

"Well, you have absolutely no credible proof that he was. You need to release him."

"I can't release him based on your say-so."

"No, you are going to have to put the case together, but if you keep focusing on Magren, as unsavory as he is, you are doing justice a disservice. And Mrs. Crewes has committed a crime irrespective of if you believe she murdered Mr. Dellow, which I am absolutely certain she did. Besides, Mr. Dellow let his assailant into his house and he'd hardly do so for Magren, would he?"

He sighed. "I'll go find the files in the morning. If what you say is true, I will arrest her—for fraud if not more. We'll see what comes out when we question her. You may well be right. Shame in a way, because I thought we finally had Magren."

"I don't think he's guilty of Mr. Dellow's murder," Dory repeated. "This is a crime related to pure greed."

"Usually more insidious," he said. The planes thundered overhead and he looked up. "Looks like you're busy. I'll leave you to your task." It seemed as though all energy had drained out of him.

A string of explosions went off behind them and they all looked around. It was going to be a messy night.

"There's a shelter down the road," Dory said. "You should go there. It's not going to be a night to stay at home."

"I sometimes stay in the cells. They're solid concrete and as solid as any shelter you can find."

"Good idea. Go before the next squadron comes. Ten minutes, I'd say, before more bombs drop."

Sunderson nodded. He was about to leave. "Good work," he said before turning away. "You have a mind for investigating. Not everyone does. Maybe it is something you should consider when the war is over. Insurers use a lot of investigators."

"Yeah, maybe," Dory said. The message was still clear. Anti-aircraft guns and the police, both places where women were not welcome no matter how good they were.

He left and Dory returned her attention to what she should be doing.

"Bloody hell, Dory. You actually solved a murder," Vera said. "And the police were chasing the wrong man all along."

"Wishful thinking on their part. Blinded them, it turns out."

"Well, I think we deserve a cup of tea," Vera said and walked over to her thermos.

"You got some tea?" Dory said, pleasantly surprised. "I'd love a cup. I spent most of the day standing in queues, if you would believe."

"And solved a murder. Amazing what you can achieve in a queue. Sadly, we've still got no food in the house."

"I'll go to the store tomorrow."

"They say they are bringing in more SPAM for Christmas."

"That will be nice," Dory said, feeling guilty because she suspected the Christmas feast she would have at Wallisford Hall would likely be more extravagant. In fact, as it was only a week away, Dory decided not to write Lady Pettifer about the day's developments so she could tell her in person. Lady Pettifer would enjoy that.

Mumbling could be heard in Vera's earpiece. "They're coming," she said and put her mug down.

Dory wound her light in line with all the others down along the river. They were coming from the southwest, it seemed.

*

A cold, wet afternoon met Dory when she woke the next day. For once, she didn't have to rush out to do anything. It was all in Constable Sunderson's hands now and Dory was happy to leave him to it. As far as she was concerned, the case was solved. She knew who'd done it, and also knew the woman and her daughter would face justice for it. Mr. Dellow would receive his justice, even if the police only grudgingly let Mr. Magren go. The justice part didn't interest her so much. It may well be that Dory didn't even have to testify at the case.

Sitting up in bed, she stretched. Nothing to do today but to stand in line at the store. With Christmas coming, the Ministry of Food would probably attempt to get them a good portion of sugar again. Apples and pears were in season, so across the country, a crumble was probably on the menu for Christmas.

With slow steps, she walked over to her small desk and drew out a sheet of paper. Her room was cold and she drew her blanket tightly around her.

Dear Capt. Ridley, she started.

I uncovered the murderer of poor Mr. Dellow. A case of greed and opportunity, and then an attempt to cover up the crime. Some people's minds seem to turn to crime in these upsetting times. It brings out both the best and worst in people.

I hope everything is well with you. I worry for you. We all worry for someone.

On Christmas Eve, I will spend the day with Lady Pettifer, and she will rapturously hear the tale of Mr. Dellow's demise, and subsequent justice. Hopefully the police have concluded their investigation by then. They will not take my word on anything, which I suppose is understandable. It surprised me how intent they were on finding guilt with Mr. Magren, the local publican and hothead. Sheer disappointment, I would say.

So now my days return to normal. This case has been a wonderful distraction from the constant worry. They tell us so little of what occurs across on the continent. The degree of secret keeping seems unnecessary. Some of it the Germans seem to find out perfectly well even with our diligent secret-keeping and we do ourselves a substantial disservice for a moot cause. I suppose you would argue with me.

She could almost hear his voice and it seemed wrong that he wasn't there to argue with her. If she could wish for one thing, it would be to speak with him. Where would he be for Christmas? Was he suffering somewhere? When they'd last met, there was a heaviness in him that hadn't been there before. She hoped it wasn't worse, and she hoped he didn't feel hopeless. Was there any hope? It was hard to tell.

In a way, she hoped she could put these thoughts down, but she didn't want to burden him with anything sounding like bleakness.

Be well, and be safe, she continued. The idea that he could be dead and she didn't even know was scary beyond belief. She wouldn't know; she wouldn't be informed. Officially, she was nothing to him other than an acquaintance, even with the tender kiss they had shared. *I will pray for you and I will think of you over Christmas. Hopefully the Germans will have the decency to leave us alone for the holidays.*

Signing off the letter, Dory folded it and pushed it into an envelope. Her heart ached whenever she wrote to him. Perhaps it was time to concede that she cared for him a great deal.

Putting the pen down, she looked around the still and quiet room. Perhaps she should get dressed and go stand in line at their local store. She'd promised to do it, so she had better get on with it. Vera and Betsy could have her Christmas rations.

Chapter 36

THE ENTRANCE HALL in Wallisford Hall was freezing when Mr. Holmes let her in. For once, he seemed happy to see her. "Miss Sparks, I trust you are well," he said.

"Yes. London is a bit of a mess, but I have fared through it sufficiently well."

"Miss Livinia said something similar."

It seemed Livinia was joining the festivities.

"Are you staying with us? Lady Pettifer was a little uncertain on the topic."

"No, I can only stay a few hours. I must head back in case… I am needed."

"I see," Mr. Holmes said. "I believe Lady Pettifer is in the parlor."

"May I take your coat?"

It seemed unusual to hand over her coat. She hardly ever took it off, even in her own house, where it was too cold to be without a coat, or wrapped in blankets. "Of course," she said and took it off. It was her dark green ATS coat, the only one she had right now. Otherwise, she hadn't worn her uniform and without her coat, was left in her skirt, blouse and cardigan. The chill immediately seeped into her clothes and she wondered if she should ask for her coat back.

Mr. Holmes let her into the parlor and opened the door to a much warmer space, where the fire was lit. Lady Pettifer sat with a knitted throw over her legs. "Dory," she said brightly. "I am so glad you made it." She didn't get up and Dory guessed that the cold was terrible on her knees.

Dory smiled as she walked over and gave the lady a kiss on her cheek. The relatively quiet week before Christmas had given Dory a few hours' sleep on the roof that night, and then a couple on the train. All things considered, she felt relatively fine, although a nap would do her good in the afternoon before she left again.

"Bring us some tea, Mr. Holmes," Lady Pettifer ordered. "I have been waiting for you, so I think we are both parched. Will Livinia be joining us?"

"I think she has gone out to exercise the dogs." Mr. Holmes replied.

"Yes, they could use a bit of a run. My brother is slowing down, I am sad to report."

"I am sorry to hear that." Dory said.

"Happens to all of us, especially this time of year. Now, tell me what news you have of your investigation."

"Well," Dory said with excitement. "I told you I found out that our victim was a Mr. Dellow. The warden who knew him said he was a quarrelsome man, confirmed by the street gossip, Mrs. Simpson."

Dory went on to tell Lady Pettifer the whole of her tale, and she gasped when Dory mentioned the letter regarding the claim, immediately linking the neighbor with the dastardly activities, much quicker off the mark than Dory had been at the time.

"How wicked," Lady Pettifer pronounced. "Claiming faux damages three months in a row and no one noticed. Unscrupulous. And then murdered the man who challenged her on it. It only goes to prove that there are some who will do absolutely anything to get their own way."

In truth, Lady Pettifer had a way of getting her own way too, although she never had to resort to anything despicable. Mostly she just expected her wishes to be complied with, and more often than not, they were.

The door opened and Lord Wallisford appeared. "I understand we are having tea. Miss Sparks, good to see you. You're staying for dinner, I take it."

"No, I can't stay. I have to get back to man my station."

"I doubt the Germans are coming tonight. I know we're not sending our planes over there." He probably shouldn't be saying that. "Christmas isn't the night to bomb anyone. One has to have some limits and understanding. I will bet the Germans won't come tonight."

"I hope so," Dory said. "We could all use a break. They have been giving us hell for months. Still, I must return in case our faith in them is misplaced."

"Yes," Lord Wallisford grumbled.

"Well, in that case, we'll have a proper luncheon and you can take my car," Lady Pettifer said.

"That's not necessary," Dory said.

"You can take it down to see your mother tomorrow, and then return it here for New Year's Eve. This is certainly a year we wish to see the end of. We started out this year together, we should finish it together." Leaning over, she clapped Dory on the knee. "Besides, I am hardly going anywhere between now and then. You could use it more than I, and I know you are a good driver."

While Dory wanted to argue the generosity, she didn't. It would save her a great deal of time having Lady Pettifer's car at her disposal. Obviously, in London, it would be more at risk, but Lady Pettifer wouldn't care about that.

"There you are. This house is infernally cold," Livinia said as she walked into the parlor. Sitting down, she poured herself a cup of tea, refusing to wait for Mr. Holmes to do it for her like Lord Wallisford did. "Ooh, mince pies. I usually can't tolerate the sight of them, but Gladys makes them edible," she said and picked one off the plate.

"She puts brandy butter in the pastry," Dory said.

"No wonder I like them," Lord Wallisford stated. "Nothing tastes more like Christmas in my book. I've heard the vicar is forbidden from ringing the bells, so it will be a silent Christmas."

Even the Christmas bells had been commandeered by the war effort. Another blanket proclamation of traditions they weren't allowed to do, but this one was understandable as the bells these days signified an invasion, and it wouldn't perhaps suit the Christmas spirit to remind people of what that would sound like.

"How is your young man?" Livinia said teasingly as she sipped her tea. She could only be referring to Captain Ridley. Seemingly, Livinia had finally forgiven him for arresting her mother. For some time, Livinia pretended he didn't exist.

"As far as I know he is well. He can't tell me where he is."

"Vivian was the same, but he's sailed for Singapore now, it turns out. He finally wrote."

"Well, he'll be safe there," Lord Wallisford said. "The Japanese will never get that far south. They have to get through China and Tibet first, and people underestimate how vast China is."

"We will all pray for a safe journey."

Even Dory would. For whatever disagreements they'd had in the past, everyone deserved a prayer for safety in this war. She also didn't wish the distress of losing a son on Lord Wallisford. Lady Pettifer would be devastated too.

"Always had a way of finding trouble, that boy, so I am glad he's out of harm's way," Lord Wallisford said.

"Is there anything on the wireless?" Lady Pettifer asked.

"The king won't broadcast his message until tomorrow. Right now there's some nonsensical man named Charlie Chaplin. Never heard of him."

"Charlie Chaplin is famous, Father," Livinia said. "From Hollywood."

"Spare me ribald from Hollywood," Lord Wallisford complained.

"It's levity, a concept you completely lack understanding for." Livinia took another mince pie off the plate. "People need a bit of levity. Brings people together."

It was strange hearing Livinia speak about what people needed. These last six, seven months had changed her perspective considerably.

"Yes, Lord Wallisford said gruffly. "Perhaps we all do. Maybe we should all dine together today. That way your aunt can join us. You too, Holmes, and

Mrs. Parsons. We should all start the Christmas celebrations today before you need to dart off this afternoon, Miss Sparks."

This was momentous. As far as Dory knew, the family and the staff had never dined together. The war was changing everyone's attitudes, it seemed.

"That would be lovely," Lady Pettifer said. "Make sure we have enough place settings for all, Mr Holmes. And bring some brandy up for the pudding."

"I will go inform Mrs. Moor," Mr. Holmes said in his ever-present cool voice.

"I'll do it," Dory said, rising from her seat. "I need to go say hello anyway." She was really glad Lord Wallisford had suggested they dine together, which meant she could have a bit of a Christmas lunch with her aunt as well. It addressed a point of discomfort whenever Dory came to visit with Lady Pettifer and Dory was asked to dine with the family. Today they were all family, and that was a lovely feeling.

The End

Next in the Dory Sparks Mysteries Series, The Summerfield Bride.

It was a surprise that Dory would ever need a wedding dress, but VE day wasn't just the end of the war, it was also the start of a new chapter—a chapter that Captain Ridley proposed they start together. A proper wedding dress, at Lady Pettifer's insistence, necessitated a visit for one of the best atelier's in London. The day proves that not all brides are equal, and Cornelia Vellsted, the Summerfield Bride, would never wear her beautiful gown down the aisle.

The Gentleman on Pennyfield Street

Printed in Great Britain
by Amazon